Arcadia

by

C. Stephen Badgley

i

ISBN: 978-0985440350

ARCADIA

Dedication

This book is dedicated to

MY FAMILY

And to all the ancestors and descendents of my parents:

Ralph Russell Badgley
1909 - 2002

and

Dorothy Pearl Hysell
1912 – 2001

Chapter I
The Storm / 20th Century

Linda, silver haired matriarch of the family, opened the door and stepped out into the back yard. She was greeted with the distant rumbling of thunder and a strong gust of cold wind, which seemed to come straight down from above her head. She gazed up at the sky in wonder. Billowing, ominous black clouds ringed the horizon. There were lightning flashes everywhere she looked.

Her two daughters Kelli and Amy soon joined her. "This is very strange weather we've been having", she said as they approached. "In all my years, I have never seen anything like this! Whoever heard of a thunderstorm in November?"

Another gust of icy wind rushed across the yard, blowing the girl's long hair about their faces. "That felt like air conditioning!" yelled Amy, a 35 year old beauty with long brown hair and deep piercing blue eyes. She was the youngest daughter.

"They said on TV last night that there's supposed to be a 40 degree temperature drop when these two fronts collide," added Kelli the oldest daughter, a lovely lady in her 40's and mother of three precious children. She also had long hair, curly and blonde like the early morning rays of the sun bouncing off the top of a wheat field.

"I just love thunderstorms," shouted Amy as she danced and twirled in the back yard. The rushing winds swirled the girls' hair around their faces. "Dad always loved them too. I wished he would come out and see this."

A bolt of lightning, which struck close by, and the resulting crack of thunder made them scurry back into the house. "That was a close one!" exclaimed Kelli. "I wish John and the kids would hurry up and get here. Casey called a minute ago and said he was on his way."

It was Thanksgiving Day and the whole family was to gather at Grandpa's house to celebrate the holiday and share family memories. Grandpa had been very quiet lately. Although he never spoke much, he seemed to be more withdrawn these days. He had not been the same old jolly fellow since he had his small stroke a few years ago. The gray haired old man was quite content to sit with his old hound dog Buddy, smoke his pipe and reminisce about the old days. He would answer you if you asked him a question but rarely volunteered to start a conversation.

His two daughters had arrived a couple days before to help their mother clean the house and prepare for Thanksgiving dinner.

Kelli had married John Renshaw and had three children, BrieAnna, Lucy and Jake. BrieAnna was the oldest at twelve, followed by Lucy at eight and little Jake at six. BrieAnna was a tomboy at heart but she is gradually changing into a very beautiful young lady.

Amy had married David Hunter and they were the parents of two precious little girls named Carrie and Adie, aged six and five.

Casey, the only son, had married Mary Ann Tyler and they were the parents of four-year-old twin boys named Stephen and Dennis.

The front door opened and in walked Casey and John with all the kids. The children were chattering and laughing like a troupe of monkeys.

"There's a big storm heading this way." Said Casey as he entered the room and sat down on the couch, "The radio says this huge cold front is moving in and causing severe thunderstorms in front of it. It's actually getting cold outside. Can you believe it was over 80 degrees yesterday?"

"The way I understand it" said John, "is that there is a cold front moving in from the north and a warm front moving in from the south and they are going to collide right here over central Ohio and us. Should be some storm; the temperature is supposed to drop down into the 30's or lower."

BrieAnna walked over to the old man and put her arms around his neck. "I love you today Grandfather." She kissed him lightly on the cheek and he smiled at her and said, "I love you too sweetheart."

All the children then followed BrieAnna's lead and gathered around Grandpa to give him hugs and kisses. Then they wandered into the kitchen to Grandma Linda and repeated the process.

The air was soon filled with chatter and laughter as the children noisily began playing games and joking with each other. The ladies were all in the kitchen putting the final touches on the dinner. The rumbling of thunder outside grew louder.

Everything was finally in its place. The tables were set and drinks poured. Because there were so many people, it was necessary to set a separate table for the children.

Grandma called the kids and they hurriedly ran into the kitchen and took their places. She then called for the men to come in and take their seats at the main table. Grandpa always sat at the end of the table. This was his place, it was his chair and no one ever attempted to sit there. He came in, nodded hello to everyone and sat down.

The table had been set with large bowls of mashed potatoes, sweet potatoes, ham, turkey, dressing, corn, green beans, cranberry sauce and Grandpa's favorite; a salad made from lettuce, vinegar and milk. His Mother used to make it for him. It was called 1-2-3 salad.

Grandma Linda asked everyone to take the hand of the person setting next to them and offered a prayer of thanks to God for all the blessings that He had bestowed upon this family. After the prayer, everyone began to dig in to this sumptuous meal.

In the beginning, the conversation revolved around the food. Those that prepared it received compliments from everyone at the table. The conversation then turned to current events of the day, such as the upcoming ball games, the war in the mid-east, the price of gasoline and the approaching storm outside.

Suddenly, there was a terrific crash of thunder. The lights flickered and went off. Casey stood up and said, "I'll go out and check the breaker switches and see if they've been tripped."

He left the table and went out to the garage where the circuit box was located. He opened the door of the box and flipped the main switch back to the on position. Nothing happened. He tried several times but no lights came on.

He returned to the table and said, "Looks like there's a power outage, because all the switches are on. There's just no power to the box. It is going to get cold in here with the furnace not working. If the power doesn't come back on soon, we'll have to build a fire in the fireplace."

One of the children, said "Oh no, we can't play computer games or watch TV. This is going to be a boring day!"

Another said, "Maybe we can play some games or something. Can we roast marsh-mallows in the fire?"

There was another loud crack of thunder and the rain began pouring down, making a loud hissing sound as it struck the roof and windows of the house.

The two fronts seemed to have met right over the top of Grandpa's house. They were like two giant armies in the sky, fighting over who was going to take control of the area. The warm front began the battle by hurling volleys of lightning bolts and sheets of rain. Its wind made a sound like the passing of so many shells. The rolling thunder sounded like cannons firing in the distance and shells exploding in the heavens.

The cold front answered the challenge with bullets of hail and its icy missiles pounded the roof and rattled the windows. It sent platoons of chilling air charging into the ranks of the warm enemy zephyrs. The result was swirling masses of turbulence, each trying to overpower the other.

Whirling dark clouds in the area of combat would drop long fingers of death and destruction towards the earth and then withdraw them before they touched down. The resulting winds had the trees whipping back and forth, power lines snapping from their poles. Blowing leaves and other debris filled the air.

Blasts of cold air raced low, as if trying to knock the legs out from under the warm front. The warm front struggled to keep its balance and hurled its might down on the enemy from above, trying to force it back north.

Amy got up and gathered some candles. She lit them and placed a couple on the tables. Then she put a few in the living room. "At least we'll have some light, it'll be dark soon."

After everyone had eaten their fill and sauntered into the living room, the women began to clean up the mess left behind. The ladies joined the men and children in the living room after they had gathered the leftovers and stacked the dishes for washing later.

Casey and John were snoring loudly as they slept off their meal. It sounded as if they were trying to harmonize with each other. John was snoring the bass parts and Casey the tenor.

Everyone else was chatting about different subjects and complaining about feeling cold. Casey and John woke up and decided it was time to build a fire. They went out to the shed, gathered a couple armloads of kindling, and soon had a good fire roaring in the fireplace.

Grandpa got up and moved his rocking chair closer to the fire. He sat back down, lit his pipe and spoke. "Listen, everyone!" All eyes turned to him and he said, "Would you all like to hear a story? I have one that was told to me by my Great Grandmother years ago when I was a little boy. I know you would all rather be watching football or playing games but seeing as how we have no power and it's too cold and stormy to go outside, I thought maybe you might like to hear this story. It's been in my head and my heart for a long, long time. It's a true story, I never told any of you before, but now's a good a time as any. I figure if I don't pass it on to you before I die, it will be lost forever."

These were the most words Grandpa had put together for quite a while and his daughter Kelli said, "Dad, we would really love to hear your story, everyone be quiet now, and let's listen to Grandpa."

BrieAnna moved over by her Grandpa and sat on the floor in front of the fireplace. The other children soon followed. The twins were both asleep. Curled up on the couch beside their Daddy, they were oblivious to the chatter in the room and the storm outside. Welcome heat and the sweet aroma of Grandpa's pipe soon filled the room.

The old man began, "As you know, I was born and raised down in Meigs County. I was born near the town of Letart Falls. Letart Falls is right in the toe of the "boot of Ohio" and I've been kicked around ever since!" He chuckled lightly.

"Why did they call it Letart Falls Dad?" asked Casey, "I never saw any falls on the river there."

"There used to be falls there a long time ago son, before all the dams were built on the river. The town carried that name because back when the area was first opened for settlement, they found the body of a Frenchman below the falls there on the river. On his arm was tattooed the name Letart. They named the area Letart's Falls or Letart's Rapids.

The river there was very shallow and quite difficult to navigate. After dams were built on the river in the late 1920's, the rapids all but disappeared. Over the years, it became Letart Falls then just Letart to some. The area across the river in West Virginia is just called Letart."

"Anyway, my Great Grandmother's maiden name was McPherson, Erissa McPherson. She was well over a hundred years old when she told me this story. Old yes, but in body only, not her mind. Her mind was as clear as a bell. She was up to date with current events and could remember even the smallest details of her life.

She showed me boxes of old letters she had kept and even let me read them. I can remember her voice yet to this day as she told me this story. I was mesmerized by it. She had a younger sister named Lorena and the story is about her; her boyfriend and a very, very special place."

The McPhersons were from up around Parkersburg, West Virginia in Wood County. The family moved to Meigs County around 1843. They settled just east of Letart Falls near the farm of my Great Great-Grandfather John Wheeler. The Wheelers and the McPhersons were farmers. They raised tobacco, wheat, corn, potatoes and other vegetables. They had cows, chickens and pigs. They ate what they grew and sold what they didn't need for cash to buy the material things necessary to live and make life easier.

There was a large meadow and an orchard between the Wheeler and McPherson farms. Both families shared the apples grown in the orchard and they both allowed their goats, cows and sheep to feed in the meadow. There was a large creek or "run" that came out of the hills and flowed past the meadow. It was and still is today, called "John's Run" because it ran through the property of John Wheeler. They would catch fish from the creek and the Ohio River to add a little change to their diet. They were self-sufficient.

Life wasn't real easy back in those days. There was plenty of work to be done just to survive. Nevertheless, they made time for fun and socializing just as we do now.

As I said before, Grandma Erissa's memory was as sharp as a tack and she was wise too. I remember her voice, so clear and firm. She had a way of talking that made you want to grab onto every word she said. When I was a child and visited her, she would tell me all kinds of stories. I have not forgotten a one of them. She could tell a story with such detail that it seemed as if you were right there in the story, watching and listening and taking part in it; just like being in a movie theatre.

She was also a packrat. She kept everything. She had old newspapers and magazines from so long ago. She never threw anything away that might have a use sometime later. She loved to read and to her, books, newspapers and magazines were a treasure.

She also loved to write letters. She sent me tons of them while she was living. I still have them, each and every one, upstairs in my "treasure box."

Those letters are a treasure to me. In those letters are memories of a life and a way of living that will never be again. Our family history is in those letters. You all can have them after I am gone. I just want you to promise me that you will keep them and treasure them as much as I have.. Well, I will try to tell the story as best I can. I know I will not be as good as Grandma Erissa's was in telling it, but I'll give it a go and hope you understand what I am trying to say.

Chapter II
Dr. J. R. Philson / Gabriel's birth July 3, 1842

Dr. J.R. Philson came out of the room where a new child had just entered the world. He went up to the father who was sitting at the kitchen table and said, "Well John, looks like you got yourself another good farm hand. A strapping boy, healthy as can be, and with a good set of lungs."

The wail of the newborn rang through the cabin. "Elva is doing just fine and will be up on her feet in just a couple of days. Make sure she stays in bed, gets some good rest til then, and make her eat. I got to be on my way now. I must check on old man Canter. He's not doing so well these days, seems to have a touch of fever from that cut he got on his leg last week."

"Doctor Philson," said John, "I want to thank you so much for comin' here and bringin' my son into this world. I promise to pay you when I get this crop of tobacco harvested and sold and in the meantime, if there's anything I can do for you, just let me know."

"Don't worry about it John, I won't, I know you'll pay me when you can."

As Doctor Philson exited the cabin, John's father Isaac met him with the doctor's horse in hand. "I done fed and watered her for you Doc; she's a fine mare you got. I want to thank you for takin care of my boy and his family."

"You're more than welcome," replied Dr. Philson, as he mounted his mare. "Stop by and see me the next time you're in Racine and I'll see if I can do anything about that bad back of yours."

The old man watched the doctor ride down the lane and out of sight. He then entered the cabin to see his new Grandson.

The other children met Papaw, (as they called him), when he entered the doorway. They excitedly proclaimed, "We got a new baby brother, Papaw, he looks like a dried up punkin. What're we gonna name him Papaw? Can we call him punkinseed? James says he's gonna be a bigun!"

"Hush, children! I'm sure your Ma and Pa will come up with a good name for him. They didn't do too bad on your names now did they?"

Rachael was the oldest. She was near ten years old, followed by James who was eight, Mark who was six, then Susan four. There had been two other children who were stillborn.

Isaac walked over to his son John and hugged him. "John, you stay here and take care of Elva. Me and the boys will take care of the chores. Rachel, you and Susie work on gettin' a good supper together for us and help your Pa if he needs you. Before we go, I want to take a look at my new Grandson."

He went into the room where Elva lay holding the new baby. "My, My, look at the size of that boy!" exclaimed Isaac. "What're you gonna call him Elva?"

John entered behind his father and said, "Me and Elva have decided to name him Gabriel Pa, after the angel Gabriel."

"That's right," said Elva, "You should have heard him a squallin' when he came out. Sounded just like Gabriel a blowin' his horn." Gabriel is a good name for him."

Isaac Wheeler was the real patriarch of the Wheeler family in Letart Falls. He was born somewhere in New York around 1780. No one knows for sure what date. When he was a young boy, his family moved from New York to Wood County, Virginia and settled across the Ohio River from Marietta, pretty close to Blennerhasset Island.

One night, when Isaac was about 10 years old, a band of about a dozen Shawnee Indians surrounded their little cabin. As the morning sun began to rise and break the darkness, his father Benjamin opened the cabin door to go outside. At that instant, the Indians fired a volley and killed him instantly.

The force of the musket balls knocked him back into the cabin where he landed on his back with his feet still protruding over the threshold. Isaac, his Mother Deborah and little sister Alana managed to pull Benjamin back inside the cabin and push the door closed. Deborah hurriedly put the wooden bolt in place so the attackers would not be able to force the door open easily.

She had little time to mourn the death of her husband. She picked up the musket that he had dropped and stood ready to protect her family. Isaac stood behind her with an old muzzle-loading pistol that had been given to him by his father.

The Indians began their siege yelling and screaming. Failing in their efforts to force the door open they began firing into the cabin through the window. Isaac was wounded in the arm and his little sister Alana was killed in the deadly hail of lead that poured through the little window.

One of the warriors tried to gain entry through that window and was halfway inside when Isaac shot and killed him. He struggled to reload the pistol as the dead warrior was pulled from the window by his fellow attackers.

Terrified, Deborah fired her husband's musket towards the window but hit nothing.

Fully in a state of panic, she threw the musket down and grabbed her infant son Jeremiah. Taking the bar from the door, she pulled it open and began to run towards the forest, clutching the infant to her breast. She didn't get very far.

The Indians chased her down and one of them buried his tomahawk into the back of her head. He then grabbed the infant by the ankles and swung him around his head. Screaming his war cry, this brave warrior smashed the baby's head against a tree. He then scalped the mother and tried to get the scalp off the dead Jeremiah. Getting only a small piece of flesh with the baby's light blonde hair attached, he looked at it, grunted and stuffed it into his scalp pouch.

Isaac, in the meantime, had managed to crawl behind some wooden hogsheads that the family used for storage and hid himself there. The Indians entered the cabin and scalped the body of his dead sister. Thinking Isaac had escaped in the melee, they didn't bother looking for him.

They began poking around the cabin. They took everything they could carry and left without discovering the crouching Isaac behind the hogsheads. He had reloaded the pistol and clutched it to his chest with the barrel under his chin. He was prepared to take his own life rather than be taken alive or killed by the savages that brutalized his family.

After the Indians left, he headed for Flinn's Station down towards Lee Creek. When he arrived he tearfully told the people there of the attack and loss of his family. A group of men were gathered and left in pursuit of the Indians without success.

Isaac was taken in by the Pickens family. They had lost a son to an Indian attack the previous year. He stayed with them until he was around fifteen then went out on own. He had grown into quite a strapping young man by then, almost six feet tall with broad shoulders and strong as an ox. He could work as hard and as long as any man twice his age.

Around 1800 Isaac decided to swim across the river to Blennerhassett Island and seek employment. He swam over easily and upon reaching the island, he built a small fire to help dry out his clothes. When they were dry, he donned them and walked to the mansion that Harman Blennerhassett had built on the northern end of the Island.

As he approached the mansion, the beauty of the lawn, the gardens and the variety of plants everywhere took him in. He knocked on the door and it was answered by a very pretty lady. "Hello" she said, "welcome to our home."

"Uh hello madam, my name is Isaac Wheeler and I was wonderin' if you might need some help around here. I'm a good strong worker and would appreciate the opportunity to work for you."

"Let me get my husband" she replied, "He may have something for you to do. Please sit over there. He'll be out in a moment." She pointed to an area where there were several cane chairs.

Soon Harman Blennerhassett came out and sat down next to Isaac. Isaac introduced himself and they talked for well over an hour. Isaac asked about the different kinds of plants and flowers he had seen growing on the island. Mr. Blennerhasset was impressed with Isaac's inquisitiveness and eagerness to learn. He hired him and Isaac spent the next two years working in the gardens and even assisting Harman in some of his botanical experiments.

It was during that time he met and married Samantha Boyce. Everyone called her "Sissy". Isaac had fallen in love with her the first time he saw her. After courting her for less than a month, Isaac proposed and she accepted. With the permission of her father, they were married and Isaac built a cabin close to where his father had built his. After a couple years of working for the Blennerhassetts, he decided to farm his own land. Isaac and Sissy had four children, all boys. The youngest one was John.

A few years after Isaac left the employment of Harman and his lovely wife, they were left destitute when they decided to back Aaron Burr in his quest to form a new country. The local militia from Marietta sacked and destroyed the beautiful mansion. Isaac always said that he believed Harman was not a traitor to his country at heart. He felt the Blennerhassets were instead victims of circumstances and the smooth talking Burr.

Around 1810 an old friend of Isaac's named Charles "Cap" Martin came to visit Isaac and talked Isaac into heading north with him to join Harrison's army.

The Shawnee Indians had taken on the appearance of going on the warpath again and Harrison had sent out a call for volunteers to help keep them in check. Actually, it didn't take much talking to get Isaac to go. He saw it as an opportunity to seek revenge for the brutal murder of his family. He readily agreed to accompany his friend against the wishes of his wife Sissy.

In 1812, the United States declared war on England and he served until the end. His friend Cap was killed at the Battle of the Thames.

While he was away, a cholera epidemic broke out and took the life of his wife and three of their children. The only one to survive was John. Isaac was devastated.

Although he had sought and gotten revenge for the deaths of his parents and siblings, he never forgave himself for not being there when the angel of death came and took his sweet Sissy and his children.

Isaac never remarried and raised John on his own. John grew up to be a lot like his father only an inch or so shorter. He had the Wheeler broad shoulders and was as strong as a bull. He married Elva Greene and he, Elva and Isaac moved to Letart Falls to settle on the land that was granted to Isaac for his service in the War of 1812. After Isaac had taken possession of the land, he signed it over to his son.

John and Isaac cleared the land of unwanted trees, scrub brush, and planted their first crop of tobacco. They soon found out that the rich soil was good for growing any kind of vegetable.

A traveler by the name of John Chapman came by one day and sold them some apple tree seedlings. He even helped them plant them in the meadow. He stayed with the Wheelers for about a week. These trees proved to be a real blessing to the Wheelers and the McPhersons when they settled nearby a few years later.

They only received one visit from the man who would later become known as Johnny Appleseed, but he left an impression on Isaac. He taught him that men should strive to "Do justly, love mercy and walk humbly with God."

Chapter III
August 3, 1844 / Lorena's birth

Dr. Philson had just arrived at the McPherson home to check on Mrs. McPherson. She was about due to deliver her child at any time. He dismounted his mare and walked up to the house. He was met at the doorway by an anxious Edwin McPherson who welcomed him and led him into the house.

They entered the bedroom where Mrs. McPherson lay. "She's havin' an awful hard time Doctor. Her water broke this mornin'. I pray you can do something."

"I'll take a look and see what I can do. Fetch me some hot water and towels or bed sheets." The family waited anxiously in the living room as the Doctor examined Catherine.

After a short while, he came out of the bedroom and walked over to ten-year-old Daniel, Ed's son. "Danny, do you know where old man Canter lives?

"Yes sir", replied Daniel.

"I want you to hop on my old mare out there and ride over to the Canters. Tell Emily that Dr. Philson needs her right away and bring her back here. Hurry son!"

Daniel bolted out the door and mounted Dr. Philson's mare. He kicked her in the sides and headed for the Canter's house, which was about a mile and a half away. Danny kept the mare at full gallop and its sides were heaving as he pulled her up to a stop in the front yard of the Canter house.

He leapt off the horse and ran to the door. He began banging it with his fist and shouting. "Emily, Emily, come quick! Come quick Emily!"

Old man Canter opened the door and said "What in the world is wrong with you boy?"

"Doc Philson needs Emily real quick. Somethin's wrong with my Ma."

"Stay here, boy, I'll fetch her for you."

He left and soon came back to the door with Emily who was clutching a bag.

"We need you bad Emily!" cried Danny. "Hop on the back of the mare with me and I'll carry you over there!"

Danny mounted the mare and helped Emily get on behind him. She clutched his waist as he kicked the mare in the sides and headed home.

As the mare and its passengers came upon the house, Emily dismounted before the mare had come to a complete stop and bounded up the steps to the door where Dr. Philson met her.

"The baby's turned wrong Emily and I need your midwife skills to help me save them both."

Emily rushed towards the bedroom and Dr. Philson said to Daniel, "The old nag's not used to running like that, walk her real slow now until she cools off. Then brush her down. Don't give her any feed or water until she stops heaving."

Danny got the mare cooled down and brushed. He gave her water and some oats then went inside the house to see what was going on.

His little sister Erissa ran up to him, he picked her up and she put her arms around his neck and began crying. She was about five years old at the time and was upset with all the confusion going on in the house. He calmed her down and then went to the bedroom door and peered in. His father took him by the arm and led him back into the living room.

"Everything is gonna to be all right Danny, the Doctor and Emily says that they are both gonna to be fine now."

The cry of a baby came from the room and Daniel asked, "Is it a boy or a girl?"

"It's a girl," Edwin told his son, "and a real beauty. Looks just like her mother. Your Ma's already named her. Her name is Lorena, Lorena Marie McPherson."

Doctor Philson emerged from the room. "Ed, both are doing just fine. Had a little scare there for a minute, but everything is just fine now. I have to move along, but I have asked Emily to stay for a couple of days to help out until Catherine can get back on her feet. She said she would. A little later on would you have Danny take her back to her house to gather some things she needs?"

"Of course, I'll take her back myself in the buggy, so she won't have to ride double. Thank you doctor for all you've done."

Ed McPherson was a quiet man, a hard worker who never turned down a request for help from anyone. He was about five foot eleven, lean and muscular. He grew up in the hills of western Virginia. He loved to hunt and fish. He knew the haunts and habits of every animal in the forest. He knew the names of all the plants and trees. He was an excellent farmer and some said he was so good he could "grow beans on a potato plant."

His only son Danny was the light of his life. He courted Catherine for over a year before he proposed to her and she accepted. They originally had a small farm in Wood County, Virginia. They lived there but a short time before he moved the family across the river to Washington County, Ohio near Belpre. He purchased the land in Meigs County, (then called Gallia County), from a man who had received the tract for his service in the war. The old soldier said he didn't want to live so close to the Indians anymore and wanted to go back east to New Jersey.

Chapter IV
Gabriel's Birthday / Lorena and the Rock /July 2, 1852

"Gabriel Wheeler! , Get your behind up here and clean up this mess you left in front of the fireplace!"

Gabriel's ears pricked up as he heard his mother calling him. "Dadburn it!" There's always somethin' I done wrong to fix whenever I wanta go to my special place. He laid down his fishing pole and ran back towards the house.

His Mother met him at the door, with her arms crossed and a scowl upon her face. "You get all them shavin's cleaned up before Pa and the boys get here for supper and then get cleaned up yourself. Look at those hands! What in the world have you been doin'?"

"Jest diggin' for some worms Ma, so I can go fishin' down at the crick."

"Well you're not goin' anywhere until you clean up that mess over there by the fireplace and get your supper. After supper, and when you get your chores done, then you can think about goin' fishin' if there's enough light out. Today's not your birthday, tomorrow is. Tomorrow's your day, not today. Now get in there and clean up that mess!"

Young Gabe had been carving on some sticks to use as fishing poles by the fireplace. There were shavings from his whittling lying all over the floor.

Tomorrow is his birthday. It has been a tradition in this family that on a person's birthday, they don't have to do any chores at all and can spend the entire day from sunup to sundown doing whatever they want to do. Gabe knew what he wanted to do; he wanted to go to his "Special Place" on the creek that ran just beyond the orchard and the meadow. This was his secret place, where he could go and let his imagination run wild.

Along the edge of the meadow was a heavily wooded area with lots of underbrush. A creek ran through the hills and wound its way down past the meadow on the other side of a huge tangle of brush and trees. Young Gabriel had found his special place by weaving his way through the dense underbrush pretending he was exploring in a jungle looking for treasure.

He was very surprised when he came upon a little clearing where the creek curved in and formed a pool. The pool was at least 25 feet across and 40 feet wide. The creek ran into the pool at one end and ran out the other. The pool was six to eight feet deep in some places.

At the edge of the creek, a very large flat rock protruded out from the bank about four or five feet into the pool. He saw the swirl of a large catfish as it sucked down a swimming grasshopper that had inadvertently landed in the water. Its struggle to swim to shore brought the catfish up from the bottom and it was soon a meal.

He knelt on the edge of the rock and put his hand into the cool water. He kicked off his shoes, sat on the edge of the rock, and eased his feet into the dark green water. This was an ideal spot for fishing, swimming and playing in general. He sat there soaking his feet and looking about at all of nature's wonders. He counted the different kinds of birds he saw flitting through the trees and listened to the different songs they were singing. The buzzing sound of dragonflies and their ability to hover fascinated him.

He watched as a muskrat ran from behind a fallen tree on the other side and slither into the water and there seemed to be squirrels darting around everywhere on the other side.

No one would be able to find this spot unless they went through the hell of finding it as he did coming through that maze of thorn bushes, brush and dead trees.

"This is a wonderful place," he thought to himself. "I'll make it my hide-a-way, my special place". He was always careful to cover his tracks when he went there so no one else could find it.

As he was running through his mind the things he was going to do on his birthday, the anticipation got the best of him and that is why he was headed for the creek when his Mother called him. He had forgotten about the mess he made and even supper. The growl in his belly brought that to mind as soon as she said the word "supper."

He hurriedly picked up the shavings off the floor and headed for the well to clean up for supper. He got to the well the same time as his Papaw Isaac, his father John and Brothers James and Mark arrived from the fields.

"Where ya been Gabe?" James asked. "We sure coulda' used you down there at the tater patch. I thought I saw you high-tailin' it up through the meadow when you thought we were just about done."

Yeah, said Mark, "I had to hoe all your weeds besides mine. It ain't your birthday til the sun comes up in the mornin'. I guess you can milk the goat and feed the hogs for me after supper, seein' as how I had to do your work!"

"Uh Uh, they's your chores!" Gabriel said. "I'm goin fishin' after supper."

In a stern voice his father John said, "Now looka here Gabe, it weren't right that you skedaddled from the tater patch. Mark and James both had to carry your end of the load. You will repay them by doin' their evenin' chores as well as your own. You can forget about fishin' until tomorrow."

After supper, Gabriel had to go out, feed the chickens, and milk the cow, which were his chores. He then had to milk the goat and feed the hogs. He also had to make sure the cows and horses had enough hay for the night. By the time he was finished it was early evening and the sun was starting to dip behind the hills. He decided to give up on the idea of going to his Special Place this day. He would go to bed early tonight and get up early in the morning.

He placed his fishing poles, his can of worms and a coil of rope next to the door so he wouldn't forget them in the morning.

As he made his way to bed, he asked his mother if he could take one of the towels with him tomorrow in case he decided to go swimming. She said, "Alright, but you'd better not leave it at the creek when you come home!" His sister Rachael said she would pack him up some food to take with him in case he wanted to stay all day.

Young Gabriel tossed and turned all night. All he could think about was going to his special place and the fun he was going to have, fishing, swimming and exploring. If he could figure out a way to get that rope up over this one limb that hung out over the water, he could pretend he was a pirate. He could swing on the rope from one side of the creek to the other and make believe he was swinging from ship to ship, like in the stories his Papaw told of the pirates of old.

Gabriel had a big catfish on the end of his line. He was trying to pull it up. His pole was bent almost double. Just as he was about to pull that big ole catfish up onto the flat rock, a flash of light appeared in his eyes and he heard his Mother calling his name.

"Gabe! Gabe! Get up! You'll sleep your birthday away!" He opened his eyes and realized he had been dreaming. The sun was shining brightly through the window. "Oh No!" he shouted as he sprung up from the bed, "I forgot to wake up!"

He hurriedly put on his pants and shirt and climbed down the ladder from his sleeping place to the kitchen. The smell of fried bacon hung heavily in the air.

His Mother said. "Sit down and have some breakfast, then you can go."

As he sat down at the table, she placed before him a plate of fried eggs, bacon and two hot biscuits.

"Rachael baked them biscuits just for you cause it's your birthday.

Rachel called out, "Happy Birthday little brother! When you decide to come home, I'll have a fresh baked raspberry pie for you."

He gobbled up his breakfast. The biscuits were so good. He smothered them with butter and took his time with those. They were still warm from the Dutch oven and he savored every bite. He washed down his breakfast with a cup of fresh milk that had been cooled in the springhouse.

As he got up to go, Rachael handed him a sack of biscuits and a small jar of honey to take with him. He thanked her and his mother and headed out the door. He was fifty feet away from the door and headed towards the meadow when he remembered his fishing poles and worms.

He turned and hurried back to the house and his Mother was standing at the door with the towel he had asked for. He gathered everything up in his arms, mumbled a quick thanks and rushed back towards the meadow.

As he neared that strip of heavily wooded area just beyond the meadow where the entranceway to his special place was hidden, he thought he heard something unusual.

"What was that?" He thought, "A bird? I ain't ever heard any birds make that kinda sound before."

He began making his way through the underbrush and as he broke out into the clearing, he heard it again.

It made the hair on the back of his neck stand up. It was a voice, a child's voice.

He laid his bundle on the ground and got down on his belly. He snaked his way forward so he could see what was making that sound.

He couldn't believe his eyes. There on his rock, in his special place, was a little girl! She was sitting cross-legged on his rock, holding a doll in front of her. She was talking to it and singing it a lullaby.

He thought to himself, "It's that dad-burned Lorena McPherson, that brat who was always a grinnin' at me in Church, pokin' at me, grabbin' my sleeves and pullin' my hair! I can't believe that she's here, at my special, secret place, sittin' on my rock, ruinin' my birthday!

He reached out with his hand and felt a rock lying just under the matted grass. He grabbed it, stood up and let it fly towards the little girl sitting on his rock. It clacked as it hit the rock and skipped into the water making a loud kerthunk!

Startled, Lorena looked up and saw Gabriel standing there with his hands on his hips. "Get outta here!" He yelled. "This is my place. You don't belong here!"

At first, she was frightened, but instantly her fright turned to anger. "This ain't your place, Gabriel Wheeler, this is my place. I found it and I was here first so you get out!"

He looked down and saw several rocks lying by his feet. He picked up a couple and started winging them towards Lorena. Her anger turned back to fright as she gathered up her doll clothes. Clutching her doll to her face, she began to run up along the creek.

With tears streaming from her eyes she cried, "You're nasty and mean, Gabriel Wheeler and I'm gonna tell my Ma on you!" She cut up over the bank and started making her way through the underbrush.

Gabriel yelled, "Go ahead and tell your Ma, it's my birthday, I can do whatever I want, and besides, my Pa owns this creek anyhow. You stay away from here! Don't you ever come back!"

Lorena emerged from the undergrowth into the meadow when her anger returned. She stomped her foot and whirled around. "He can't do that to me", she thought, "I can give him just what he gave to me!"

She laid her dolly down on the ground and quietly made her way back down towards the creek. When she came out into the clearing, she saw Gabriel standing on the rock getting ready to fish.

She reached down, grabbed a rock, and hurled it with all her strength in his direction. Clack! Kerthunk! went the rock as it struck right next to Gabriel and bounced into the water.

He turned around and yelled, "Get outta here! I told you already you don't belong here!"

She let go another rock and it wasn't even close. He yelled up at her again, "I ain't scared of your rock throwin; you couldn't hit the broad side of a barn if you were standin' in it!"

She let go another one and it sailed over his head. He turned to watch it hit the water and when he turned back around to yell another insult, a rock struck him right in the head.

His eyes were huge as he looked up at her in surprise. Then the blood started to flow. He put both his hands up to his forehead, when he brought them back down and looked they were covered with blood. His eyes rolled into the back of his head and he fell backwards into the creek with a loud splash.

At first, Lorena was happy that her throw was true and felt he had gotten just what he deserved, but when she saw the blood trickle down his face, she became frightened. When he fell backwards into the creek and disappeared under the water, she became terrified.

"Oh no!" she thought, "I done kilt him!" She took off running towards the flat rock. She got to the edge and dropped down on her knees. She scanned the water but could see no sign of him. Tears streaming down her face, she bent over and reached down into the water to see if she could feel him and pull him up before he drowned.

Suddenly, the water erupted as Gabriel kicked off the bottom and came to the surface. As he came up, he grabbed the arms of the startled Lorena and pulled her into the creek with him. He dunked her under the water then let her go.

As she surfaced sputtering, he came up in front of her. She looked at him and exclaimed, "I thought I'd done kilt you!"

He replied, "You can't kill me...hurt like the dickens though, I didn't think you could throw that good!"

The rock had hit him on top of his head, making a small scalp cut that bled profusely. She said, "Let me see" and reached for his head.

At first, he pulled away then he let her put her hand behind his head and she tilted it forward. "It's just a little cut." She said. Then without warning she put both hands behind his head and dunked him hard.

He came up sputtering and tried to grab her. She ducked under the water and swam away from him. She circled around behind him while underwater and came up as he turned and splashed water in his face.

"How'd you learn to swim like that?" He asked.

"My Daddy taught me to swim when I was just a baby. I can swim better than you Gabriel Wheeler!"

"Well let's have a race then!" challenged Gabriel. "We'll start on the rock and swim three times to the other side and back, first one done...wins." She agreed and they climbed back up onto the flat rock.

As she began to take off her dress he asked, "What are you doin'?"

Standing there in her pantaloons and a cotton shirt she said, "I can swim faster without that dress holdin' me back."

He took off his trousers and as he was standing there in his long johns, she started laughing. "You sure do look funny standin' there in your underwear!"

"So do you", he replied, "Now let's get started." They moved to the edge of the rock. "On the count of three...One...Two...Three... GO!"

They both dove into the water at the same time and began to swim frantically towards the opposite shore. Until the first turn back towards the rock, they were side by side. Then Lorena began to pull ahead a little. By the time they made the second turn, she was ahead by a full body length. When he reached the rock the final time, she was already sitting there waiting on him.

As he pulled himself up onto the rock, he said, "I give up, I guess you can stay, but you gotta promise me one thing."

"What?" she asked.

"Promise me you won't tell anyone at school that you beat me swimmin'."

She said, "I promise."

"What's that big ole rope for?" Lorena asked.

He explained to her how he was going to tie it to that big limb that was hanging overhead so he could swing out over the water.

He looped the end of the rope around his waist and walked over to the big tree. He looked up and exclaimed "Whew, this ain't gonna be easy! That's a long way up there!"

He jumped up, grabbed a low branch on the tree, and began to pull himself up.

"Be careful!" shouted Lorena, you just might fall and break your neck!" "I'll try to catch you if you fall."

"You just stay back!' he replied. "I'll be alright, I'm a good climber, you just keep that rope from getting' tangled up in somethin."

He reached the overhanging limb and lying on his belly began to gingerly inch his way out over the creek.

"Whip that rope up over those bushes and move out on the rock" he told Lorena.

She worked the rope up over the bushes and holding the end walked out on the flat rock.

Gabriel carefully untied the rope from around his waist and looped it over the tree branch. He attached it to the limb by using seven or eight half hitches.

"That should do it. Give it a try Lorena."

She took a few steps backward and darted towards the end of the rock holding the rope. She leapt out and swung almost clear to the other side of the pool. "Wheeee!" She yelled as she began her backward swing. About halfway back, she let go of the rope and landed in the water with a splash. She surfaced and called up to Gabriel. "That was sure fun Gabe! Come on down and you try it."

Gabe began to inch his way back towards the tree then hesitated. He looked down at the water below him as Lorena yelled up to him.

"Jump from there Gabe!"

"It's too far!" he replied.

"You can do it, don't be askeered. The water's deep here."

Gabriel reluctantly slid off the limb but held on with both hands. Dangling there, Lorena prodded him to let go.

"Come on Gabe, do you want me to come up there and get you?"

Gabe's pride overcame is fear and he let go of the limb. Arms and legs flailing he fell on his back into the water with a loud splash. It felt as if someone had smacked him between his shoulder blades. He kicked off the bottom and surfaced next to Lorena.

Sputtering and gasping for breath he managed to blurt out, "That was sure somethin!"

Lorena grabbed the rope and started to swim towards the rock. "Come on; wait til you try the rope!"

They had a great time swinging, swimming and diving off the rock. Playing pirates, they captured many ships and collected all kinds of treasure. They forgot all about fishing. Gabriel had even forgotten about the biscuits and honey he had brought along. When Lorena complained of being hungry he remembered them and said, "C'mon up here, I got some good stuff, biscuits and honey."

Of course, something else had found the biscuits first. They were covered with ants. They tossed the biscuits into the water. "The catfish will eat 'em," said Gabe.

It was getting to be late afternoon so they decided to head for home. Gabe with the thoughts of raspberry pie in his head and Lorena with the thoughts of a new found friend.

Before they departed they each took an oath that neither one of them would divulge the location of their "Special Place."

"Cross my heart and hope to die, stick a needle in my eye." They promised to meet here again this Sunday.

Chapter V
The Ball Game / Naming of Arcadia / The Storm

They met again that Sunday and every Sunday they could from that time on. They had become very good friends. Of course, Gabe's family wondered where he was off to every Sunday after dinner. Sometimes he wouldn't even finish his dinner and asked to take it with him.

"Why are you in such an all-fire hurry to get outta here? His brother James asked one especially hot Sunday afternoon.

"Cause it's hotter than a fourth o' July firecracker and I want to go swimmin!" Gabe replied.

"And who ya goin swimmin' with?" Mark inquired. "Do you want me to come along with you? I could use a swim myself."

Mark looked at James and said, "Maybe we should both go. I ain't been swimmin' for quite a spell."

Papaw looked over at John and added, "What say ye John? Why don't me and you go along with the boys and see if we can catch us a mess of catfish for supper tonight?"

"No!" shouted Gabe. Desperately trying to think of an excuse for them not to come he blurted out, "I just want to go alone, uh...I need time to be by myself so I can... uh, think and clear my head!"

Amid the laughter that ensued, his Mother said, "Seems to me like you've done a powerful lot of thinkin'g already! Your head seems pretty much cleared out. You forgot to put up your Sunday clothes when we got back from Church. They're still wadded up on the floor by your bed. And I hope you haven't forgotten how to wash the dishes, the clothes and cleanin' up the house, because tomorrow's Rachel's birthday and you'll be doin' her chores as well as your own."

The look on Gabriel's face brought another round of laughter. James took sympathy on his little brother and said, "Don't worry Gabe; we ain't goin to go with you and spoil your fun. Me and Mark already told the Sayre boys we would play on their team today. You should think about comin' into Letart with us sometime and playin' Town Ball. We have a great time."

"What is this Town Ball you boys are always talkin' about?" asked Papaw. Is it some kind of a dance or somethin'?"

"No Papaw, it's a game, a game made up of two teams who try to score more points than the other does. Whatever team makes the most points wins the game."

"Is it like Tag or Hide & Seek?"

"No, Papaw, Nathan Sayre, says it's an "Athletic" event."

Papaw asked, "Well how do you play this here athletical event?"

"Well Papaw, you choose up sides or teams. Each side can have as many players as wants to play, but no more than 15 players on a team. If you get more than that, you just keep runnin' into fellers."

"There are four or five safe bases dependin' on where we play. If we play over on Hugh Adams's place, we have five bases. If we play near the school in Letart, we only have 4 because it is a smaller place."

"Each team picks a Captain and the Captains decide on how many "Innings" are to be played dependin' on the time of day. It is called an "inning" because when a team gets to bat they are "in at bat." The other team is playin' in the field and they try to get the other team out."

Papaw scratched his head and said, "Now you got me really confused! In? Out?, Chasin' bats?"

"No, Papaw let me go on! When a team is "in at bat", one of their players stands by the "Home Base" and holds a bat or big stick. He is called a "Batter" or a "Striker."

"The other team has a man standin' 50 feet in front of the "Batter" or "Striker" and he throws an India rubber ball towards him. The Batter tries to hit the ball with his stick and then run to the first base before the ball can be recovered and thrown between him and the base or thrown and hit him."

"If he can get to the base before that happens, he can either stay there or try to run to the next base without bein' crossed out or hit with the ball. He can keep his foot on any base he reaches and stop if he wants to. He can't be put out as long as he is touchin' a base. The next batter may be able to advance him by strikin' the ball."

"The object of the game is to make it to each base without bein' crossed out, tagged by someone holdin' the ball, or hit by a thrown ball. When you make it back to the home base, you score a point, or run."

The players on the team that is "at bat" take turns bein' the batter or striker and until each of their players is "put out," they continue to bat in turn. Once a player is "put out," he can't bat again durin' that inning."

"There's more than one way to put a player out. If the player is the "Batter" and he swings his stick at the ball but fails to strike it he is "put out" after his third try to hit the ball."

"If he strikes the ball and it rolls on the ground, one of the fielders can pick it up and throw it at the player as he runs to a base. If he hits the player, the player is "put out".

"If he throws the ball and it crosses the path of the player between him and the base, he is "put out". This is called bein' "crossed out".

"If a fielder picks up the ball and runs to the base or throws to another fielder at the base and the base or the runner is touched by the ball before the runner gets there, the runner is "put out".

"If a batter hits the ball up in the air and the ball is caught either on the fly or after one bounce, the batter is "put out".

"Once everyone on a team that's at bat is "put out" the teams switch places and those who played in the field now get to take their turns "at bat." Do you understand the game now Papaw?"

"I'm not sure," said the old man. "John, let's me and you go into town and see what this is all about. Maybe I could understand it if it saw it."

John looked over at his wife and asked, "How about it Elva, you, Rachael and Susan want to come along with us into town and see this here ball game? It sounds real interestin'."

"I'd love to John", Elva said. "Susan, go get your bonnet. Rachael, you too."

"I don't think I'll go Mama," said Rachael, "I'll stay here and do up the dishes then read a little."

"You better come along." said James, "Last Sunday Job Gloeckner was there and Missy Brewer was makin' eyes at him all day!"

"What makes you think I care anything about Job Gloeckner? I don't give a hoot nor a holler about him! What was Missy wearing anyway? Did he make eyes back at her? I guess I will come along and see what this is all about too."

Mark said, "Last Sunday there were a lot of people there to watch us play. Some even had picnic lunches and old man Cross was a sellin' roasted peanuts in paper sacks."

Gabriel was sure glad the subject switched from him going swimming to an outing in Letart. He was certainly glad he didn't have to explain why he was going to the creek to play with Lorena.

He could just hear his brothers teasing, "Playin' with a girl? You sissy you! Gabe's got a girlfriend! Gabe's got a girlfriend!" He could imagine the ridicule he would get from them and was sure they would tell his friends at church and school. His life would be miserable.

Of course, he could tell Lorena to stay away, but there was something about her that kept drawing her to his mind. She was as much a boy as some of his friends at school. She could outrun and outswim even him.

"She can definitely throw rocks", he thought as he rubbed his fingers across the small scar on top of his head. She knew the names all the animals, fish, birds and insects at their Special Place. Said her father taught her all about such things.

He had learned a lot from her. He enjoyed being with her. He could talk to her without being put down. She listened to him and he loved to hear her talk. She was a special person to him and he didn't want anything to happen that would end their friendship.

That particular Sunday at Lorena's house, her family had also decided to go into Letart to watch the ball game. Danny was going to play on the Sayre team also.

Erissa wanted to stay home with Lorena but Lorena didn't want her to. Lorena said she wasn't feeling well and urged her sister to go along with the rest of the family.

After the dinner dishes were washed and put away, Lorena watched the family ride off in the wagon towards Letart. As the horse turned at the end of the lane, she took off through the orchard to meet Gabriel. When she reached the Special Place, he was already there, waiting for her.

"Did you bring the worms?' she asked as she approached him.

"No, he replied, "I forgot 'em."

That's all right," she said, "I forgot my fishin' pole anyway. Let's go swimmin' then we can play pirate or go down by the riffles and look for gold."

"Come sit with me for a spell," said Gabriel, "I want to talk to you about somethin'."

She went out on the flat rock and sat beside him. They moved to the edge of the rock, took off their shoes and put their feet into the cool water.

"You know, since I found this place..."

"WE found this place!" she loudly interrupted.

"Alright, since we found this place, we've been comin' down here for the longest time. We ought to come up with a name for this place. I don't know about you, but I have had the best times in my life here, bein' with you. You're my best friend and it seems like this place was made just for us. What do you think?

"You're right" she said, "I never want to be anywhere but here. There's so much we can do here, so many fun things to do, and doin' 'em with you makes it all the better. You're my best friend too. I can talk to my sister Erissa, but there are some things I only want to share with you."

"Me too" said Gabe, "Seems like every time I try to talk to James or Mark they always end up pokin' fun at me, or tell me to go ask Pa or Papaw so mostly I tell things to you alone, I know you won't make fun of me."

She looked over at him and said, "You know, I think I love you, Gabriel Wheeler."

"I think I love you too Lorena McPherson."

"Mr. Story came over to the house yesterday to borrow a saw" said Gabe, " I was talkin' to Mrs. Story about Heaven, you know, what we was talkin' about in Sunday School Class last week. She's very smart and knows a lot about everything.

She said there are different names for Heaven like Paradise, Utopia, and Nirvana and so on, but one name she told me I really liked. She said the ancient Greeks called it Arcadia. She said that they described it as a place in the woods where it was peaceful and quiet, filled with all kinds of animals and different plants and flowers. She said the Greeks believed that their God Zeus was born there and it was a mystic place."

"I asked her what mystic meant and she said that it means sometimes, strange things happen there. I thought it was mighty strange that I would let you, bein' a girl and such, come into my secret place then of all things, become my best friend."

"Don't forget, it was my secret place too!" Lorena said. "How'd you think I felt that day you scared me by sneakin up on me and chuckin rocks at me. I was so scared at first, and then I was mad. I hated you for a little bit. I think it was strange that I turned around that day and came back and when you pulled me into the creek, I could have wrung your neck. I don't know why I came back, just mad I guess, but I'm glad I did. So, let's name this place Arcamia."

"Not Arcamia! It's Arcadia!"

"Oh, she said, "Arcadia. Hmm, Arcadia, I like that name."

"Let's go swimmin' now," said Gabe. They stood up and walked to the back of the flat rock they had been sitting on. They removed their outer clothing and Gabe took off running. When he reached the edge of the flat rock, he did a somersault and cannon balled into the creek. Lorena was right behind him.

They dove under the water and as they met, they grappled with each other playfully. They surfaced with her in his arms. Laughing he began to tickle her and she grabbed him around the neck and tried to force his head under water. They were laughing, playing, and having a great time.

They paused for a second to rest and they held onto each other while treading water, Gabe looked into

Lorena's dark blue eyes and for a moment their eyes locked and their laughs stopped.

As Gabe stared at his friend, an urge to kiss her came over him. He had never felt that way before and couldn't resist. When his lips met hers, she pulled away and shouted, "Why'd you do that for?"

"I don't know" he replied, "I'm sorry, I won't ever do it again. You just looked so pretty, I don't know what came over me."

She looked at him with eyes wide and said, "Gabriel Wheeler, if you ever do that again... She paused and made her way over to him. "I'll kiss you right back!"

She lunged at him, grabbed him around his neck, and forced his head under water. As he came up, for air, she pulled his head towards her face and kissed him full on the lips.

They pulled themselves up on the flat rock and began to dry themselves off. As they were putting their clothes back on, Lorena happened to look up into the sky.

"Look!" She said, "There's a storm comin!"

There were black clouds swirling through the azure blue sky. They heard the distant roll of thunder and the wind began to pick up.

"We'd better head home," Gabe said. "Looks like a bad one comin!"

Suddenly, the air seemed filled with electricity as a lightning bolt cut across the sky. There was a loud burst of thunder followed by another flash of lightning. "Come on, let's go!" shouted Lorena.

"Wait a second, said Gabe and held up his hand to hush Lorena. "What's that noise?"

He stared up towards the woods where the trail he and Lorena had made through the thicket came to the edge of the clearing. "What is that? "Someone's comin'!"

Making his way through the trail they had formed through the brush was the strangest little boy they had ever seen. He was wearing blue trousers and a bright yellow shirt with some kind of markings on it. He was wearing glasses and his shoes were white! He hadn't seen Gabe and Lorena yet.

Gabe said, "Come on Lorena, let's run him out of here!" They both grabbed some rocks and started throwing them and shouting at the startled little boy. He screamed as one of the rocks bounced off his shoulder and struck him in the ear.

Holding his ear, he ran crying back up the trail and out into the meadow. There was another flash of lightning followed almost instantly by a crack of thunder.

"Who was that?" asked Lorena.

"I don't know," replied Gabriel. "I ain't ever seen him before. I don't think he'll be back though. Lorena you can chuck rocks better that anybody I know. You caught that boy right in the side of the head!"

"I hope I didn't hurt him too bad." said Lorena, he was hollerin' like he was either hurt or scared to death didn't he?"

"Yeah, like I said, I doubt if he'll ever come back here again."

Just then, the sky opened up and the rain began to pour. Gabe and Lorena said their goodbyes and started running towards their homes. Gabe stopped and turned. He shouted, "Remember Lorena, Arcadia!"

"Arcadia! Arcadia forever!" Lorena shouted back.

Chapter VI
Pickin' Apples / The Fight / October, 1858

It was a special time of the year. The apples in the orchard that was shared by both the Wheelers and the McPhersons were ready for picking. There would be fresh apple pie, fried apples and most importantly cider.

John and Isaac had built a cider press in an outbuilding and once all the apples were picked, both families would process the ones selected for cider making. The liquid refreshment was to be shared evenly.

Now fresh apple cider is a wholesome and refreshing beverage but it was a well-known fact that Papaw Isaac Wheeler preferred his cider to be aged and hardened. As a matter of fact, years ago he had the cooper in Racine make an oak barrel just for him. When the cooper was finished with it, Isaac took it to a woodcarver who lived in the small town of Plants and had him carve his name into the barrel. The barrel said "The property of Isaac Wheeler."

On the day of harvesting, the McPhersons and Wheelers met in the orchard. Danny McPherson led an old horse who pulled a small two-wheeled cart to the orchard. Edwin walked along side and his two daughters Erissa and Lorena rode in the cart. The Wheeler clan was already at the orchard when they arrived that morning. Gabriel went to the cart and helped Erissa and Lorena climb out.

"Howdy Ed." said Isaac, are you ready to get started? How's the wife these days?"

"Yes sir, I'm ready and she's doin' pretty well. She's headed over to your house a little later on to help Elva and Rachel get ready for some pie makin. She's cartin' some glass jars she got from old man Cross. They're gonna try to make somethin' called apple butter. She got the recipe from Granny Gloeckner over in Letart. Supposed to be some real good eaten I hear."

"Why you wearin' your brothers pants? Gabe asked Lorena.

"You don't think I'm gonna climb up them trees wearin' a dress do ya? You ding-dong!

"Are you gonna climb this year?"

"I would have climbed last year if Pa would have let me." I can climb as good as you can Gabriel Wheeler!

"No doubt about that!" Erissa exclaimed. "Well she can climb if she wants to. You'd never catch me up in one of them trees. I'd fall for sure and probably break my dang neck."

She looked over at Mark and mouthed a kiss toward him. Startled at first, Mark waited until no one was looking and sent one back towards Erissa.

John said, "Mark you bring our horse and cart over here and we'll start gatherin' the apples off the ground. Erissa you and Susan pick up the apples that bounce out of Danny's cart."

"Ed, you, Pa and me will start pickin up the ones on the ground and put 'em in Mark's cart. Let's get started."

Danny waited until his father, Isaac and John had picked up all the apples off the ground and them in the cart. He led his horst to the next tree.

Gabriel, James and Lorena began to climb up into the tree. They picked the apples hanging on the branches and tossed them into the cart below. Some stayed in the cart, some bounced out. The ones that bounced out were gathered by Erissa and Susan and placed back into the cart.

Some of the apples couldn't be reached so the pickers would shake those branches and the apples would tumble to the ground. Erissa and Susan also gathered these also.

As they moved from tree to tree, they talked about different things. Danny hollered up and asked Gabriel, "Hey Gabe, how's your head? I heard old Stoney's out to pay you back."

"It'll be a cold day in hell afore I run from that bullheaded buzzard. Let him come on!"

A few weeks earlier, James and Mark had talked Gabriel into playing in one of their ball games at Letart. The Sayre team was playing the Stobart team. Stoney Stobart was the Captain of the opposing team and when Gabriel was at bat he began taunting Gabriel.

Gabriel hit the first ball that was thrown and Stoney Stobart fielded it. As Gabriel was running towards the base Stoney threw the ball as hard as he could and it caught Gabriel in the back of the head, knocking him to the ground.

Nathan Sayre, Captain of the Sayre team, ran over to help Gabriel up. He yelled at Stony, "Why didn't you throw at his legs?

"Hell!" replied Stoney, "I was throwin at his ass! Looks like I hit what I was throwin' at too!"

Of course smarting from the blow to his head and taken aback by that remark, Gabriel charged across the field with the intent of bashing Stoney down.

Before he could get to Stoney, James & Mark wrestled him to the ground. "Just take it easy Gabe, It's just a game. Don't pay any attention to him. Don't let him make you get throwed out of the game!"

Well Stoney kept taunting Gabriel. Calling him names and saying he played ball like a girl and such. When the Stobart team went to bat, one of their players hit the ball towards Gabriel.

Stoney was still taunting Gabriel. Gabe fielded the ball and instead of throwing the ball at the runner, he turned around and threw it at Stoney. His aim was good and it caught Stoney right in the mouth.

In an instant Stoney bolted onto the field spitting blood and running towards Gabriel. Gabriel stood his ground and as Stoney lunged for him, he sidestepped, grabbed Stoney by the collar of his shirt, and flung him to the ground.

Nathan Sayre ran over and was yelling, "Boys, boys, stop this right now, we can't..." Another Stobart boy jumping on his back and knocking him to the ground cut his words short.

There ensued one of the biggest melees ever seen in these parts. Players from both teams and even some of the spectators flooded the field. Fists, feet and cusswords were flying everywhere!

The three Wheeler brothers and Danny McPherson formed a square with their back toward one another and successfully whipped anybody who tried to get to any one them.

Isaac and John were sitting in the grass laughing at the spectacle. John looked over at Isaac and said, "Looka there Pa! Just look at my boys protecting one another. Ain't that a sight to see?"

"Oh my, that had to hurt," said Isaac as someone went running at the boys with a bat in his hand. Mark waited until he was as close as could be and ready to swing the bat while on the run. Mark then dropped down and swung his legs at the attacker's legs. His maneuver worked and the attacker went sprawling onto the ground among the other three defenders. A kick to both sides of his ribs by James and Gabriel, followed by a kick to the head by Danny, put this feller out of commission quickly.

"Do ya think we ought to go in and get them out of there before one of 'em gets hurt Pa?"

"Naw, let 'em have their fun. Now this is what I call an "Athletical" event. Might go in and join 'em here myself in a little while."

The Town Constable, with a little help from some local citizens, finally got everyone separated and calmed down. The participants, some carrying their fallen comrades, limped home and the Constable shouted, "If this ever happens again, there'll be no more ball games in this town!"

The families finished harvesting the apples and went to the Wheeler house. The women and girls began peeling apples to make the pies and apple butter while the men began to press their cider.

They used a very large iron kettle in which they placed the apples and began to pound them with a heavy maul to reduce them to what was called pomace.

The pomace was then wrapped in linen and placed in a wooden frame forming what they called a "cheese." These "cheeses" were then placed in the press and two 40 foot long, extremely heavy, wooden pressing beams were lowered by levers to press the juice from the cheese.

The juice would flow by means of gutters to be collected in wooden tubs. The juice was strained again through linen cloth or cheesecloth into wooden casks or barrels. The pomace that was left over after the squeezing was divided up between the families and used as feed for their hogs.

When they were finished, Mark and Erissa decided they wanted to take an evening stroll together. James said, "I'm gonna ride over to the Norris place and visit for a while. Gabriel knew what was on James's mind.

"Gonna go see Maggie ain't ya?" It was well known in the area that James and Maggie Norris had been courting.

Gabriel whispered to Lorena, "Let's me and you go to Arcadia for a while, maybe take a swim."

She smiled at him and said, "Look here Gabe, I got an apple pie I made just for me and you. Let's take it with us. We'll eat it there."

Chapter VII
Arcadia / Plans to marry and build a home /Brothers marry

Grandpa paused in his story telling long enough to knock the ashes out of his pipe. He refilled it with his aromatic tobacco and the family waited anxiously for him to continue.

The storm outside was still going on and showed no signs of letting up. Lightning would make the room flash with an eerie light as if someone outside was taking pictures with a flash attachment and the thunder would rattle the windows. The light from the candles and fireplace made them feel cozy, safe and warm. They were enthralled by Grandpa's story and pressed him to continue.

Over the years, the relationship between Gabriel and Lorena blossomed into a full-blown love story. People around the area learned of their relationship, because they were always together. They also learned of their special place called Arcadia and respected Gabriel and Lorena enough never to go there unless invited; even his brothers.

Gabriel and Lorena widened the trail to Arcadia through the underbrush and Lorena planted all kind of flowers and ornamental bushes around this special place. Gabe began clearing the brush out and before long; it was what could be called an actual paradise.

The flat rock that jutted out over the water was their usual meeting place. The area behind it had all been cleared out and they talked about someday building a house there.

Everyone who was invited to visit Arcadia was in awe by the sheer beauty of the place. In the summer, it was always cool there no matter what the temperature was or how high the humidity was.

The wintertime painted a different picture. The pool would sometimes ice completely over except for the far side. The ice being thick enough to support the weight of several people, Lorena and Gabriel would invite some of their friends to come over from time to time and go sleigh riding and build a huge bonfire.

After sleigh riding and playing on the ice, there would be singing and games played around the fire. In the cold evenings, the moon light would reflect off the snow-covered hills making them take on an eerie bluish glow.

Many of their friends fell in love there and one couple even asked if they could be married at Arcadia. Of course, Lorena and Gabriel told them that this was not possible.

Although Gabriel had never officially proposed to Lorena, it was assumed by both of them and everybody else that they were to be life mates and would marry someday. That marriage would take place at Arcadia, their special place.

Rachael married Job Gloeckner and was the mother of three children who they named Martin, Helen and Laura. They lived pretty close to Letart Falls and Job worked on one of the riverboats that hauled cargo and passengers up and down the Ohio River.

James got married in December of 1858. He married Margaret Norris who he had been courting for some time and in September 1859 they had a child, a little boy whom they named Albert. Margaret, whom everyone called Maggie, had been ill with consumption for some time and died in 1861. She was buried in the little cemetery at the far end of the meadow where John and Elva had buried two little babies that had been stillborn. James and little Albert moved back into the Wheeler home.

Mark, my Great Grandfather, married Erissa, who he had been courting for a while, and they built a small house along the river near Apple Grove. They had two children, the first one they named John. They called him "Little John." The youngest boy was named Isaac and they called him "Little Isaac." I guess they called them "little" to distinguish them from their Grandpa John and Great Grandpa Isaac. "Little John" was my Grandfather.

William Simpson who lived in Antiquity was courting Susan. He also worked on the riverboats.

Chapter VIII
Lincoln elected / Escaped Slaves / November, 1860

Abraham Lincoln of Illinois has been elected the new President of the United States. He won the race for office over Democrat Stephen A. Douglas of Illinois.

The Democrat party had split during this election with the northern Democrats nominating Douglas. They held that congress had no power to either sanction or forbid slavery in the territories such as Kansas and that only the people who lived there should have the choice.

The southern Democrats had nominated John C. Breckenridge of Kentucky as their candidate. They held that it was the express duty of congress to sanction and protect slavery in all the territories of the republic and maintained that the constitution, in its own right, carried slavery into them.

The Republicans nominated Lincoln and denied all intention to interfere with the domestic institutions of the states of the union, but were determined to prevent the introduction of slavery into the territories by congressional legislation and denounced as false the assertion that the constitution established slavery in any part of the union.

The southern states had threatened to secede from the Union in the event of the election of a president hostile to slavery. On December 17, 1860, the state of South Carolina adopted an Ordinance of Secession and on the 20th, they withdrew from the Union. Georgia, Florida, Alabama, Mississippi, Louisiana and Texas soon followed them. Later on in the year, Virginia, Tennessee, North Carolina and Arkansas joined the Confederacy.

The southern states that had seceded formed a new government called the Confederate States of America and elected as their president, Jefferson Davis of Mississippi. Their capital was Montgomery, Alabama.

There was talk of war in Letart Falls and around the county. There were some who were in sympathy with the southern states that had seceded, but they were the minority. If the union were to be saved there would have to be armed conflict to bring those states back into the union.

The postmaster at Letart Falls was a staunch Unionist. It was found out that he was holding all letters passing through his office going to the southern states. After threats of lynching, he finally agreed to let them pass.

On May 23, 1861, Virginia seceded from the Union. On June 11, 1861, the western counties of Virginia withdrew from the State of Virginia and announced their intention of forming a new state and remaining in the Union. This included Jackson and Mason Counties, which are right across the river from Meigs County, Ohio. Not all residents of western Virginia were happy with this decision and they remained loyal to Virginia and the Confederacy.

At first, they were going to name this new state Kanawha, but later decided to call it West Virginia.

The President made a call for 75,000 men to assist in putting down the rebellion of the seceding states. Patriotism permeated the area. The people became animated with the spirit. Their battle cry was "Down with the traitor, Up with the flag!"

The Wheeler and McPherson family were caught up in this patriotic fervor along with everybody else. They knew that the main issues of the upcoming conflict were preserving the Union and slavery. They had never been slaveholders themselves, but they knew several people across the river who were slave owners.

They were always against slavery. Once, years ago, John had found a black man and two black women hiding in the meadow near the orchard. When he asked them what they were doing there, they told him they were trying to go north to freedom. They had escaped from their owner over in Virginia and were terrified that they were about to be caught.

The man said, "Las night, I heard them dogs a barkin'. I know the Massa has done sent his slave catchers to get us. Theys close...real close and I don't know where to go or what to do. Can you please help us mister?"

John felt compassion for them and led them to the house where Elva fixed them a meal of cornbread, bacon and fried potatoes. Isaac placed some boards in the rafters of their tobacco shed and after they ate, John supplied them with some blankets and water and had them climb up in the rafters to hide while he and Isaac figured out what to do.

Later that afternoon the McPhersons came over for a visit. John told Edwin about the slaves he had hiding in the tobacco shed and asked for help in figuring out what to do with them.

Ed said, "Tomorrow morning, I'll come over with my wagon. We'll put them in the back, cover them with some tobacco, and take them to the Giles farm over near Rutland."

"I was over there a few times to buy seed and once while talkin about the evils of slavery, Ole man Giles told me he helped escaped slaves get north to Canada. He told me his farm was a station on what's called an underground railroad. He warned me not to tell anyone, but he said if ever I had the chance to help a slave get north to freedom, just come to him. Now's the time I reckon."

The McPherson's were invited in to share the evening meal and as they sat at the table, their conversation was interrupted by the baying of hounds off in the distance, beyond the meadow.

Isaac got up and said, "Looks like them slave catchers are a comin' this way. I'll deal with 'em, you & Ed watch my back. Elva, you & Catherine stay in the house."

He went over the fireplace and took his old pistol down from the wall. He always kept it there. An old flintlock pistol was that was given to him by his father. He had used when he fought in the War of 1812. It was his most prized possession. He charged it with powder, rammed a lead ball down the barrel, and went out on the front porch to await the slave catchers.

John and Ed armed themselves with an old musket and a Kentucky Long Rifle that John used to hunt deer. John climbed up to the roof of the house and hid behind the chimney. Ed hid himself just inside the doorway.

It wasn't long before three mounted men came into view. A black man followed them on foot, struggling to hold onto the leashes of two Redbone coonhounds. The three men pulled up their horses in front of the porch.

They were a motley looking bunch. They were all filthy. Each had a shaggy beard and they were armed with pistols and rifles. One spit out a chaw of tobacco and it landed on the porch step. He looked at Isaac and said, "We're lookin fer three niggers that took off from John Smalley's place. We been sent to fetch 'em back. They's a buck and two wenches, you seen 'em ole man?"

Isaac didn't answer or even acknowledge the presence of the slave catchers. He just sat there in his chair and with a piece of cloth, wiped the barrel of his pistol.

"Are ye deaf ole man? I'm a talkin to ya!"

Isaac looked up and said, "If you're a talkin' to me, then I suggest you get your ass down off that horse. I don't talk up to no man, especially the likes of you!"

"Ain't you sumpthin' ole man, all high and mighty?" I bet you're one of them damned abolitionists. Ifen I hafta climb down from this horse, I might just kick your sorry ole ass all over that porch!" This brought a guffaw from the other two riders.

"Try to do that," Isaac said sternly, "and I'll put a ball right twixt your eyes."

"You're purty stupid ole man; you can't get all three of us with that there single shot blunderbuss yer a packin'."

"Don't need to get all three of you." replied Isaac calmly. "But you can be damn sure I'll get you."

"That's right." said Ed as he stepped out on the porch and leveled his musket. "And I got a bead on the big feller to your right."

"And I got one on the other!" yelled John from the rooftop.

The two riders looked at their leader nervously and one said, "C'mon Sam, let's git!"

Sam turned to him and said, "No! Mr. Smalley's payin' us good money to fetch his property back."

He turned back to Isaac and said, "Now I know you fellas seed them niggers. My dogs tracked them right to here. Now where are they?"

"There ain't no darkies here", said Isaac. "Them mutts of yours probably picked up the wrong trail, probably follerin' an ole coon scent."

"No sir!" Said Sam, "My dogs don't hunt coons; they hunt niggers and they're damn good at it. Now I know them niggers are here abouts. We'll just have us a look-see."

"Listen you muddle headed fool!" said Isaac angrily as he stood up and leveled his pistol at Sam, "There ain't no runaway darkies here, I done tole you that.

You'll get your stinkin butts and those mangy mongrels off of my property right now if you want to see another sunrise!"

The slave catcher could see the anger in Isaac's face and the fire in his eyes. He knew he meant what he said.

"We'll git for now ole man, but we'll be back. The law's on our side. We'll go and fetch the sheriff and then we'll have a look-see here."

As the slave catchers slowly rode away with the slave dog handler trying to keep up, the black man glanced back at Isaac. He smiled and waved his hand, being careful not to let the slave catchers see him do it. Isaac lifted his hand and returned the gesture.

"Maybe we ought to take 'em to Rutland right now," said Ed, "Those boys will be back with the Sheriff tomorrow."

John thought for a moment then said, "You go on home Ed, "Get a few hours sleep, I'll bring 'em over to your house and we'll leave from there around midnight. To get the sheriff, those boys will be travelin' the Bashan Road to Chester. We'll take the river road through Racine and Syracuse. That way we won't cross paths. By the time they get back here from Chester, we'll be on our way back from Rutland."

John and Ed took the slaves that night and got them to the Giles farm near Rutland and the next summer, Old man Giles told Ed that those particular slaves made it safely to Canada.

Perhaps it was Isaacs's fiery rhetoric and determination he showed or maybe the slave catchers decided that their chosen trade was just too hazardous. Whatever the reason, they never came back with the sheriff. And they never were seen in those parts again.

Old Isaac spoke often of the slave dog handler. He wondered and hoped that he would find his freedom someday also.

Chapter IX
The Pendant / Proposal /June, 1861

The night sky was so clear that you could see every star in the heavens. The light from the moon was so bright you could almost see to read outside.

Gabriel and Lorena took a walk to Arcadia to sit on their favorite rock and soak their feet in the cool water. The still night air was broken only by the sounds of the creek gurgling and the occasional hoot of an owl in the woods across the pool.

In the distance could be heard the howling of a coon dog as it tracked its quarry through the woods. Soon the howls turned to yelps and Gabe said, "Sounds like he got his coon."

He reached over, put his arm around Lorena's waist, and pulled her towards him. He kissed her lightly on her forehead and ran his fingers through her long brown hair.

She put her head on his shoulder and sighed, "I wish there wasn't a war coming. I just know you're gonna go and get yourself killed or wounded." I can't bear the thoughts of losin' you."

"Lets not talk about that now," said Gabe, "I got a present for you."

"What is it?" she asked?

"First let me tell you how I came about gettin' it.

"It was early this spring, I had come down here to Arcadia, and you weren't here yet. I walked down to the riffles where we used to pan for gold when we were children and for some reason I had to urge to reach into the water. I grabbed a handful of sand and rocks off the bottom. When I pulled my hand up and opened it, there was this beautiful, flat, red rock lying in the palm of my hand. I'd never seen anything like it before. It was shaped like a heart. I felt around for a while but never found any more. It was a dark red and very shiny. It looked almost like glass. I didn't tell you about it because an idea came to my head.

"I took it to Mr. Brinker, the watchmaker, in Racine and he told me it was some sort of crystal. Not valuable like a diamond or ruby, but beautiful anyhow. I saved up some money and he made a gold frame around the edges for me and made a pendant out of it."

He reached in his shirt pocket and pulled out the pendant. It was attached to a gold chain. He placed it around Lorena's neck. As she held the pendant in her hand, she began crying.

"What in the heck are you cryin' for?" asked Gabriel. "I thought you'd like it. Look, it even has our names carved real small in the frame. It says, "Gabriel's heart for Lorena, Arcadia 1861." "I want you to have this Lorena, because on this night, I am askin' you to marry me. I want you to have my real heart forever."

"Oh Gabe, she sobbed, "Of course I'll marry you. You are my life. I couldn't' imagine any type of life without you."

"Then its settled." he said, "All I have to do is get your father's permission and we can set the date."

He pulled her back and they lay on the flat stone staring up at the night sky.

"When we marry Gabe, I want to name the first boy after you. I want a "Little Gabe" and I want to name the next boy after your father and then the next after my father. We'll name the girls after our mothers. I want lots of children. I want to raise them right here in Arcadia."

"My Pa told me that this place is ours forever, Lorena. James and Mark said they would help me build a house right here for us. Pa says we can use part of the meadow to farm and I've saved up almost enough money to get us started. Life will be sweet with you always by my side Lorena."

Shooting stars would dart across the dark sky every once and a while. They would watch them and say Money! Money! Money! real quick. When they were young, Papaw Isaac had told them if you could say Money, Money, Money before they burned out you would become rich some day.

All of a sudden, a large meteor broke through the atmosphere. You could hear the hissing and see the red, green and orange sparks flying off the tail as it streaked through the sky. An eerie greenish light permeated the area for an instant.

Gabe and Lorena forgot to say the magic words as their attention was taken by this spectacle. They both sat up. "What was that!" cried Lorena?

"It was a meteor," said Gabe. "Papaw says whenever you see a big one like that it means someone you know has passed away."

Chapter X
4th Regiment West Virginia Infantry / The Brothers Enlist

Almost everybody from eastern Meigs County was at the town of Racine to celebrate the 4th of July. There were drums banging right along with the firecrackers. The fifers were playing as Ephraim Carson of Racine, Britton Cook, Thomas Barton of Syracuse and William Brown of Pomeroy were recruiting for the 4th Regiment of West Virginia Infantry. They had a recruiting booth set up covered by banners of red, white and blue. Men were standing around singing:

Yes, we'll rally round the flag, boys, we'll rally once again,
Shouting the battle cry of Freedom,
We will rally from the hillside, we'll gather from the plain,
Shouting the battle cry of Freedom.
The Union forever, Hurrah! Boys, hurrah! Down with the traitors, up with the stars,
While we rally round the flag, boys, Rally once again,
Shouting the battle cry of Freedom.

There were lines of men and boys waiting to sign up to preserve the Union. "We won't be long. It won't take no time to kick those rebel asses back in line." "Ole Abe will make sure this is quick work." "And when this is over, what'll you think will happen to all the niggers down south?" "Reckon they'll go back to Africa." "You ignorant ass, some of them don't even know what Africa is." "What makes you think they wanna go someplace they don't even know?" "Maybe, they'll come up here and live with you?" "Ain't livin with me, hell, I can't hardly feed my own young'uns let alone someone else's." "Ole Abe'll figure out what to do with 'em." "When we gonna get our uniforms and what kind of guns are we gettin'?" "Hell boy, you ain't' even signed up yet! They'll probably make you wear a dress and carry a broom anyway" "Hey, Thomas, Thomas Lewis, what're you doin in this line? You ain't old enough to go fight! You gotta be over 18 to enlist boy." "I am over 18" "No you ain't, I remember when your ma whelped you."

Thomas took off his shoe and pulled out a piece of paper. He unfolded it and showed it to his accuser. It had the number 18 written on it. "See, I put this in my shoe and when they ask me if I'm over 18 I can honestly say, yes sir I am! I'm a goin' and that's that! "Now leave me be and mind yer own business!"

In one of the lines were the Wheeler brothers, James, Mark and Gabriel along with Daniel McPherson. James was still in mourning for the loss of his wife Maggie. She died the night Gabriel proposed to Lorena. Gabriel hadn't told anyone about the meteor he and Lorena saw that night. Perhaps it was just a coincidence. He knew Papaw would harp on it so much and out of sympathy for his brother, he decided to let it lay.

James looked at his brothers and said, "You two should really consider not joinin' up right now. Mark you and Erissa have those two boys that need you, and Gabriel I know Lorena is very disappointed you postponed the weddin'. Why don't you two just go back home and take care of your loved ones? My little Albert will be fine with his grandma and grandpa. You boys have your whole life ahead of you. I'll take care of doin' the family's part in this war. You shouldn't be goin'."

He paused for a second. "Think about it Gabriel, in the time you are goin' to be away, you and Mark could have that house built down at Arcadia and you and

Lorena would be startin' your family. And Mark, you know Erissa wants another child. She told me the other day she would give her right hand if you would just stay at home."

Marked looked at his older brother and said, "You ain't gonna talk me out of goin' with you James. Me and Erissa are still young and we have plenty of time to make more children when I get home."

"Same here," said Gabe, "You know I love Lorena more than anything, but we can build our house at Arcadia after we get back. Besides, I want you there to help. There's no one who can lay out a plan for a house like you. And you know all the ways to make it just right. I feel it's my patriotic duty to serve my country same as you James. Now please don't bring it up again, me and Mark are goin' with you and that's that!"

There was laughter in the lines as young Thomas Lewis received a boot on his bottom from one of the soldiers signing up the men. "Git outta here kid and don't even think about commin' back until your old enough! You ain't even been weaned yet and you ain't allowed to take your mama!"

The boys signed their names on the line and it became official. They were now Privates in Company E, Fourth Regiment of West Virginia Infantry. They were to report for mustering in on July 22 at Mason City, West Virginia.

Chapter XI
Papaw Isaac / Mysterious Happenings at Arcadia / July 19, 1861

The McPhersons came over to the Wheeler's house and the women were preparing a feast for their boys who were leaving tomorrow for Mason City. Erissa and Lorena tried to hold back the tears as they prepared the table. After the meal, the men went out on the porch to smoke and drink a little hard cider.

Papaw Isaac went to the shed and got his special keg. Isaac was getting up in years and had a touch of senility. Drinking hard cider seemed to aggravate his condition and after a few glasses he would sometimes say things that didn't make much sense or drift back to his youth and carry on about events and places in his past. By the time the women came out to join the men, he was on his third glass.

"Dang it! I sure wish I was goin' with you boys. If I could just get my legs to work, I think I could keep up with you. I was a good soldier once."

"I remember back in 1811 when I was with Harrison at Tippecanoe. Them injens were plumb crazy! They was told that they were invincible and that our bullets would just bounce off them. They kept comin at us and we kept cuttin' 'em down. You see, they were told by "The Prophet", one of their leaders, that they were gonna kill us all and that they were under some divine spell. "The Prophet" was the brother of Tecumseh. If Tecumseh had been there, they never would have attacked us."

"I heard that after Tecumseh returned he nearly kilt his brother. The British made Tecumseh a general and we fought his Shawnee warriors again at The Thames in 1813. They fought differently that time. They are sly devils. They sneak up on you. They listen for you to fire your musket, then two of them will rush you with their tommy hawks raised and screamin' like mad men. They know it takes some time to reload and figure they can get to you before you can get another ball in your musket. The screamin' was meant to rattle your nerves and make it hard for you to get your musket reloaded."

"That's why I carried that old pistol I got. It saved my life a few times. He paused for a moment then said, "What's that? Is that a rooster a crowin'? What's got into that fool chicken! It ain't even mornin' yet! He paused again then looked at the boys sitting on the porch. What are you boys doin sittin' here? Ain't you got chores to do?"

"Pa," John said, we got no chores today. This is a special day; the boys are goin off to war."

"Goin' to war? What in tarnation! How come nobody told me about this here war? Hell, I'll get my gun and go with you! Have I ever told you about the fightin at Tippecanoe? Well, I was up there with Harrison back in 1811...

"Pa", you just told us about that. Why don't you go in and take a nice afternoon nap?"

"That sounds like a good idea," Papaw said as he struggled to get out of his chair. Gabriel quickly got up and helped his grandfather to his feet. "C'mon Papaw, I'll help you."

Isaac turned, looked at him and said, "Thank you John, you're a good son."

"I'm Gabriel Papaw!"

Isaac did a double take, squinted his eyes and looked again. "So you are, so you are. You're a good son too."

Gabriel helped his grandfather into the house and returned to the porch. He sat down on the porch step next to Lorena.

Mark and Erissa excused themselves saying they were going for a walk. James put little Albert on his shoulder and said, "Come on, let's go for a ride!" He took off jogging down the lane with little Albert holding onto his head for dear life, laughing and giggling as he bounced on his daddy's shoulders.

"Let's go down to Arcadia for a while." Gabriel said to Lorena. She nodded yes and Gabriel turned to the others and said, "We're goin' down to Arcadia for a little while. We'll be back soon." Hand in hand, they walked towards the meadow.

"How old is your Pa John?" asked Edwin.

"He was born way back durin' the Revolution Ed; somewhere up in New York. He don't remember the year. My Grandpa came down and settled near Parkersburg way back. Indians killed both my grandparents."

"Pa married my mother and had me and four other children. All are dead now. Cholera got 'em. When Elva and I married, Pa, her and me came down the river and settled here."

"He got this land from bein' in the war. This land will be passed on to the family when Pa and I are gone. What do you think of my boys Ed?"

"Mark is a fine son-in-law. He treats my Erissa very well and has given me two fine grandsons. I expect Gabriel will make me a fine son-in-law too. I know them two's been together since they was children. I know Gabe will treat Lorena like she should be treated. He's a fine young man."

"I wish this war would never have happened. I fear for my boy Danny, He's the only one I got to carry on the family name."

Elva said, "Ed, Danny is in our prayers just as much as our boys." The Lord will watch over them and bring them back to us. You'll see. Just put your faith in Him. Danny's like a brother to our boys and you know they all look after each other."

"Catherine looked up at Elva and said. "You know Elva, I s'pect your right about that. I believe that the

Lord created Gabriel and my Lorena for a special purpose. Ever since Lorena was a little girl, all she ever talked about was Gabriel! Gabriel this and Gabriel that! Gabe kissed me today and so on and so on. He's been such a big part of her life that I don't think the Lord would be so cruel to keep those two apart. And I can tell he loves her as deeply as she loves him. They were meant for each other."

"And that place, Arcadia," Catherine continued, "I think he created that place for them. Have any of you noticed anything strange about that place? In the summer, when it's as hot as can be, with no wind a blowin', it's always so cool and breezy down there. Why is that? And in the wintertime why don't it freeze over on the other side. It's like the Lord keeps the water open over there so all the animals can get a drink."

John sat his glass down on the porch and said, "I asked Pa that once and he said, he reckoned that the way the hills are standin' there and the way they channel the air down past Arcadia makes for a constant breeze and with the water in the creek constantly flowin' it makes it cooler. He said if you combine that with all the trees around givin' shade it's no wonder it's always cool there. I guess that makes sense so I never questioned it further.

As far as the other side never freezin' over, that's where the main channel of the creek is. Flowin' water doesn't freeze easily."

"I know that's true..." said Ed, "but I've seen the creek frozen over solid both above and below Arcadia yet that far side has never froze. There was no water runnin' into or out of Arcadia."

"What I'd like to know," interjected Elva, "is how in the world Lorena gets all those different kinds of flowers to grow down there. I've even seen sunflowers down there over six feet tall and a growin in the shade!"

"I'll tell you something I have never told anyone before" said Catherine, "because it kinda scared me and you might think I was crazy."

"Once a few years ago, I went down to Arcadia lookin' for Lorena. She wasn't there so I was just lookin' at all the pretty flowers she had planted. I went over to this red rose bush and decided to cut some of those roses to take back to the house with me. I thought they would look pretty settin' on the table. I cut about a dozen and noticed some yellow roses a little ways off. I decided to cut some of them too."

"As I was walkin' over there, I thought to myself, "I hope Lorena doesn't get mad cause I took some of her roses." I glanced back at the red rose bush I had just left and I couldn't believe my eyes. It was as if I hadn't taken any roses off that bush at all."

"I took quite a few of the yellow roses, as they are my favorite, and there weren't many left on the bush. I started walkin' home and glanced one more time at the red rose bush. I was still puzzled. I then glanced back at the yellow rose bush and that was when I became frightened. The yellow rose bush was full of yellow roses again, just like the red bush. It was as if I had never taken a rose off of either one of them!"

"I hurried back home and have never been back to Arcadia by myself since. Do y'all all think I'm' crazy?"

"No I don't" answered Ed, "I had a strange experience down there myself. Once I went down there to do some fishin'. I was sittin' on that flat rock tryin' to catch a mess of catfish. These two little otters started playin' on the shoreline across the pool. I was watchin' these two little critters and laughin' at their play. One of them had a small white patch on his back. I think it was a male, because it was a little bigger than the other one. It was sure funny the way they would run up on the bank and then slide down into the water. They would wrestle with each other, and chase each other.

They were havin' a wonderful time and so was I just sittin' there watchin' 'em."

"All of a sudden, this big red tailed hawk swooped in, grabbed the one with the white markin', and flew off with it. The little one stood up on its hind legs and watched the hawk make off with its mate."

"I was furious at first. If I'd had a gun with me, I would have taken a shot at that hawk. That hawk could have had his choice of any kind of bird he wanted and I was so upset that he took that little otter." He paused for a second.

"Anyway, after a while I got over it, I reckon a hawk's gotta eat too. About an hour later, I heard a splashin' sound and looked across the pool. There were those two otters again! The one with the white patch was back and they were playin' again, as though nothin' had happened! I was mystified. I watched them for a while before I took my fish and went home in wonderment of it all. I never did figure out how that otter got away from that hawk and came back."

Gabriel and Lorena arrived at the trail leading down to Arcadia. They stopped at the top and gazed down at their paradise. A doe was coming down the hill on the opposite side, leading her fawn to the pool for a drink. She ignored the couple completely. Gabriel and Lorena watched the fawn drink from the pool and laughed as it slipped and almost fell in.

The doe looked up at the as if to say to them, 'Hush, he's just a baby!" She then led the fawn back up the hill and as she started to go over the top, she turned again to look at Gabriel and Lorena for an instant before she disappeared into the forest.

As they approached their flat rock, a bullfrog let out a croak and jumped into the water. A pair of mallards glided silently in out of the sky and settled on the pool. A bluegill tried to snatch a water spider out in the middle of the pool and caused a splash. As the spreading circles of its action moved out over the surface, the two mallards swam over to investigate.

Bees and Butterflies were flitting around the flowers Lorena had planted. There were the little white ones and the orange and black Monarchs.

Humming birds came and drew sweet nectar from the flowers she had planted. Brilliant red Cardinals flew in and out of the pine trees that Gabriel had planted along the eastern side of the pool. Blue Jays, Yellow Finches, Robins, Blackbirds and Sparrows could be seen busily flying back and forth to their nests in the trees.

Squirrels were playing in the woods across from the pool, scampering along the forest floor and scurrying up the trees chasing one another. They would leap from tree branch to tree branch, then down one tree trunk and up another in a never-ending game of tag.

A pair of otters scrambled down the bank and slid into the water. There was a pleasant breeze blowing along the creek, which, combined with the shade of the huge trees all around, made Arcadia as cool as being inside a springhouse.

As they sat there on their rock watching all the action around them, Lorena held out her hand to Gabe and said, "Here, I have something for you to take with you." In her hand was a small soft leather pouch. On the outside of the pouch there was a hard leather tag sewn on that had the following words burned into it by Lorena's brother. It read: "Gabriel Wheeler, Letart Falls, O. from Lorena at Arcadia 1861."

Gabe took it and opened the drawstrings. Inside were 100 silver 3-cent coins. "I want you to keep this and use the money to send me letters with."

"Thank you Lorena, I promise I'll write as much as I can."

She clutched the pendant she wore around her neck and said, "Gabe, I know you're gonna run into other girls while you're away and I want you to know if temptation should arise and you fall, I will forgive you. I just pray that you'll come safely home to me."

"That thought has never entered my mind, Lorena; you're the only girl for me. God created you for me and I promise to you and swear to him right now that I will never have anything to do with any other girl. My heart belongs to you only. Whenever you think of me while I'm gone, just look at that pendant and you'll know I'll be thinkin' of you. Our day to be together forever will come, sooner or later; I know in my heart that you and I are destined to be together forever."

"I feel that way too Gabe. I promise you here and now that I will wait for you, no matter how long it takes. I will never be anyone's wife but yours. I will look forward to the day you come home to me, when we can get married and start our family here at Arcadia. I know that God has meant us to be together and he provided this place for us to share. I know that he will make sure you get home to me. It's only a matter of time. I pray it will be a short time."

Gabriel wiped away a tear that was streaming down Lorena's cheek and kissed her gently. "We'd better go back to the house now." They stopped at the top of the trail and looked back at Arcadia. "I'm definitely gonna miss this place while I'm gone. We've had so much happiness here."

"It'll be the same when you return Gabe; I won't let the weeds and brush take it over." It will be as beautiful then as it is now." Hand in hand, they walked through the meadow and orchard back to the house.

The sun was beginning its westward slide towards the horizon as they approached the house. Both families were sitting on the front porch waiting for them to return. Papaw Isaac was still in bed and probably would remain there for the night.

"We were just about to come lookin' for you," said Mark, "thought maybe you had drowned or somethin'. Come on up and have some cider."

Erissa handed them both a glass of cider and as Gabriel took his, he said," This ain't Papaw's stuff is it?"

James, who was sitting on Isaac's barrel laughed and answered, "No sir, looks like Papaw's done drained his barrel. He's in there snorin' away."

John looked at his sons and said, "Boys, let me tell you somethin' about your Grandpa. His age has caught up with him. His mind ain't what it used to be, but I can tell you this, if he was in his right mind, he'd be out here right now, and if he was in his younger days, he'd be goin' right along with you in the mornin'. There'd be no one who could stop him."

"He's had many tryin' times in his life, been through hell and back and lost a lot of friends and loved ones along the way. Just as I am, he has always been so proud of you boys and the fine young men you turned out to be."

"He's always been a strong man both physically and mentally and I pray those qualities are instilled in each of you. When you go into battle, be strong, but be smart too. Before you do somethin' that'll put you in harm's way, think before you act. Don't try to be a hero. Your Grandpa would tell you that. I know he'd also tell you to remember your loved ones that are back here waitin' for you and that we need you to return to us."

"I know you'll see death in its ugliest form. Boys, your grandpa never spoke a lot about his experience in the war and how it affected him, but the few times he did talk to me about it I could tell it is not somethin' easy to live with. War is not like one of your ball games you used to play when you were lads. You're gonna be up against someone who is gonna to try his best to kill you. You boys will need to look after each other and watch each other's backs. You very well may have to take the life of another man. Be strong, do what you have to do to protect each other and survive. These are the things that your Papaw would tell you if he were able to."

As the sun went down behind the hills, James said, "We'd better get some rest, come sunup we've got a long walk ahead of us."

Everyone hugged and kissed each other as the McPhersons gathered in the yard to leave for the McPherson home. Erissa was staying with Mark at the Wheeler home. Lorena and Gabriel embraced and expressed their love for each other.

Between her sobs, Lorena managed to say, "I love you Gabriel Wheeler, you listen to what your Pa said and be smart and come home to me."

"I will Lorena, I love you so much. I'll be home as quick as I can." He stood and watched as Lorena and her family headed towards the meadow. He wiped the tears from his cheeks with his handkerchief. He called out Lorena's name, "Lorena! Lorena!" As she turned he shouted, "Arcadia!"

She stopped, turned around and waving her hand over her head shouted back, "Arcadia! Arcadia forever!"

Chapter XII
The Departure / The Trip to Mason, West Virginia / July 20, 1861

As the rooster crowed it's welcome to the morning sun, the boys woke up and got out of bed. The house was filled with the aroma of fresh coffee and breakfast. Their mother and sisters had been up for quite some time, preparing a huge breakfast. The men were going to sit down to a breakfast feast the likes of which they had never seen before. The women had fried potatoes, eggs, fried apples, bacon, sausage, gravy, biscuits, butter, honey, apple butter, raspberry jelly, fresh milk and coffee.

Papaw Isaac had gotten up earlier to relieve himself and when he returned he asked, "What are you all doin' up?" They told him that they were preparing breakfast for the boys. Isaac said, "I wish I could join 'em but I ain't got no appetite at all. I ain't a feelin' so well this mornin'. Reckon I'll go on back to bed for a spell."

As he started to go out the front door, Susan took him by the arm and said, "C'mon Papaw, your bed's this way." She led him to his bed and helped him get into it. As she tucked the blankets up around his chin, she kissed his forehead and said, "Good night, Papaw." He mumbled something then turned over on his side.

Rachael had spent the night at her parent's home and prepared several batches of her biscuits in the Dutch oven. She placed a lot of them in a cloth bag for the boys to take with them on their way to Mason City. She included a jar of raspberry jelly and a jar of apple butter.

As they sat down and began their breakfast, there was a knock at the door. Erissa opened the door and there stood her brother Danny with a knapsack tossed over his shoulder.

John said, "C'mon in Danny and have some breakfast."

"No thanks Mr. Wheeler, I done ate at home, but I will take some coffee." He sat his knapsack down on the porch and entered the house. He hugged his sister and kissed her on the forehead.

"Oh, and I will have one of Rachael's biscuits. I always got room for those and maybe a little apple butter on it."

Catherine said, "Well just sit yourself down and help yourself to whatever you want. We got plenty."

"Thank you Mrs. Wheeler, Mark, pass the butter will you please."

Gabriel asked Danny about Lorena.

"She was up most of the night cryin' and when I got up, Ma said she had given her somethin' that Doc Philson had given her a while back to help her sleep. It sure worked good. She didn't even wake up when I kissed her goodbye. She's restin' real good right now."

Gabe dropped his head at the thought of his beloved Lorena.

"Don't worry Gabe," Danny said, "they's talk that it won't take long before this rebellion is put down, them Johnnies are just as anxious to get this over with as we are and once they see we ain't gonna stand for disunion, they'll give in and we'll all be comin' home before you know it."

"Reckon so," said Gabriel as he took a sip of coffee. "Sure hope so."

"We'll we'd better get started." James said as he got up from the table. "We got a long way to go."

Another round of hugs, kisses and tears preceded their departure. Each boy went into Papaw's room, kissed the old man on the forehead, and said their goodbyes. As James reached down to smooth his grandfather's white hair, the old man looked up at his three grandsons and in a moment of lucidity said,

"There's no such thing as a "fair fight" in battle. Do what you have to do to protect yourself, your brothers and your friends. You have to be able to count on each other when things get bad. You got to look after and depend on each other. When the balls start flyin' and there's screamin' and hollerin', smoke and gore all around you, you can't depend on anyone but yourselves. Always be alert, don't let them injuns sneak up on you and catch you unawares."

He paused for a moment as the lucidity faded. "What're you all standin' around here for? I ain't feelin' too good today, I'm gonna lay here a while until I get to feelin' better. You all go ahead and get started threshin' that wheat. I'll be out to help later on. Go on now git!"

The boys threw their knapsacks and the sack containing Rachael's biscuits over their shoulders and headed down the lane towards the road that led to Letart Falls. There they would pick up the river road and follow it down through Plants, Antiquity, Racine, Syracuse, Minersville and Pomeroy to the ferry where they would cross the mighty Ohio River to Mason City, West Virginia.

Not to long ago it was called Mason City, Virginia. Not all the people in the western counties were for secession from their mother state and many slaveholders and others vowed to take up arms against the Unionists and preserve their affiliation with the great state of Virginia and the Confederate cause. Many friends and families were torn apart because of their beliefs, on both sides of the River.

The people of Meigs County, Ohio and Mason and Jackson County, West Virginia could almost all claim roots to one side of the river or the other. There were Union Regiments formed in West Virginia that recruited heavily on the Ohio side of the river. There were Ohio Union Regiments that were formed who recruited on the West Virginia side also.

The Confederacy also recruited heavily in Mason, Jackson and Kanawha Counties and formed units such as the 17th and 19th Virginia Cavalry and the 22nd Virginia Infantry.

As the boys passed through the village of Antiquity, they were joined by the Adams brothers Isaac and Gilbert. "What ya got in that bag?" asked Mark.

"Got me some salt pork and cornbread for our supper tonight. What you got?"

"We got some biscuits, apple butter and raspberry jelly."

"Maybe we can share some of our vittles tonight" said Isaac, "I got a taste for apple butter and biscuits."

As they entered the town of Racine, they stopped to rest for a spell under the shade of a large sycamore tree. A young man approached them and inquired where they were headed. When they answered Mason City he said, "I'm headin' that way myself to jine up with the 4th West Virginia Infantry. My name's Thomas, Thomas Wolf, my friend Pete Lallance is supposed to meet up with me here." James introduced himself and his brothers. Isaac and Gilbert introduced themselves.

James said, "We'll just sit here for a while and wait on your friend then we can all go on together."

Thomas said, "They's a lot of fellers from these parts goin over there. I s'pect there were 20 or 30 passed by here yesterday. They's more from Gallia and Athens Counties joined the 4th too. My Pa said he'd come along if he didn't have to stay and tend the store. "Looka here what's in my tote bag he gave me to take along!"

Inside the tote bag was 25 to 30 pound smoked ham. "If you all will help me tote it, I'll share it with you."

"Yessir Thomas, we'll help you tote it alright," said Isaac. "We're gonna have a purty good supper tonight. I'm gettin' hungry right now just thinkin' about it."

"Here comes Pete now." said Thomas.

"Look at that feller!" Said Gilbert, he must be ten feet tall!"

Across the field walked a tall, thin man wearing a stovetop hat, which made him appear taller than he actually was. As he came up to the group Thomas said, "Fellers, this here's Pete Lallance. Pete this is the Wheeler brothers, James, Mark and Gabe, this here's Danny McPherson, and these two here are the Adams brothers, Isaac and Gilbert.

Howdys were said all the way around and Isaac stood up next to Pete. As he looked up at him he asked, "Jest how tall are you mister?"

I'm six feet, nine inches" said Pete, "and I'm still growin'."

"My word! Ole Abe ain't even that tall! I'm five feet nine and I been told I was tall! It's a real pleasure to meet somebody I can look up to!" He shook Thomas's hand and said, "Let's head 'er on down the road boys. We got a ways to go."

Isaac said jokingly, "Can I wear your hat Pete, so's I don't look so small?"

As they walked along, Gabriel took out the pouch that Lorena had given him and was looking at it when Gilbert asked, "What ya got there?"

"A gift from my fiancée"

"What's her name?"

"Lorena, Lorena McPherson."

"Any relation to your friend Danny there?"

"Yep, his sister."

"Lorena, that's a right purty name. When you gonna marry her?"

"Just as soon as I get back, got to build us our house first."

"Where you plannin' to settle when you get back?"

"Got us a nice place already. It's such a wonderful place. Lorena and I found it when we were just children. We call it Arcadia."

"Is that a town? Never heard of it."

"No, it's a place, a place near my father's farm. It has a creek that runs into it on one end and forms a large pool of water. The creek runs out of the other end over a series of rocks and riffles. There are beautiful wooded hills across the pool and a big meadow behind it. Lorena and I cleared it all out years ago and she's planted flowers and all different kinds of plants around it. We're gonna build our house just above the creek and farm the meadow behind it. My Pa has already told us we could have that land and my brothers are gonna help me build the house."

"Sounds like you got it all planned out, I wish you happiness there and I hope we all get home soon so's you can get started on it. Why did you name this place Arcadia?"

"Arcadia is another name for Heaven. It's a Greek name. To me and Lorena it is like Heaven so we picked that name."

"Now I know who you are!" exclaimed Thomas, "I heard my folks talk about you and your girl up at Letart. Folks come in to the store and talk about you and her and that special place you have. What was that name? Arcania?"

"No, Arcadia," replied Gabriel. Arcadia with a "d".

Pete, who caught the last part of the conversation said, "Arcadia, that's the place where Zeus was born. Zeus was a Greek God. There was another Greek god named Pan who actually took care of the place. It was like a wilderness paradise full of nymphs, strange plants and animals. Pan took care of them all. Strange things happened there. I studied Greek mythology for a while."

"Isaac asked," What in the world is miffology?"

"Mythology is the study of something that is not real. The ancient Greeks believed it was real though. They had all kinds of strange beliefs. This god Pan for example, had the upper torso of a human, but the lower part of his body was that of goat. He had horns like a goat and he played the pipes. He was the son of Zeus and a nymph."

"What's a nymph?"

"A nymph is a shadowy female being of nature. Nymphs live in mountains and groves, by springs, creeks and rivers."

"I ain't never seen no nymphs. Wouldn't know one if I did." Isaac.said.

"That's because they are a part of mythology, a myth, they don't really exist, they are a part of what makes up a good story."

"Do you know this story? asked James, whose interest was caught by the conversation. "If you do, maybe you could tell us this story sometime to help pass the time away."

"Pete's good at tellin' stories." said Thomas. "Once he gets started though, you can't shut him up! He'll keep you up all night!"

The group of men passed through the villages of Syracuse and Minersville. There were other groups of men, some walking, some on horseback, on the road in front of them and some could be seen a distance back. Occasionally a rider or a wagon would approach them coming from the direction they were heading. They were asked if they were going to Mason City. "Sure are a lot of you fellers goin' over there!" One rider said. "Must have passed 40 or 50 men since I left Middleport this mornin'. All goin' to Mason."

As they neared the edge of Pomeroy, Mark said, "How bout if we find us a place to bed down for the night. We can get up early and cross over the river tomorrow. Won't take us too long to get to the ferry from here."

"That sounds like a good plan to me." said Isaac, "I'm plumb tuckered out and nearly starved to death!"

The hills above Pomeroy formed cliffs that came straight down to a small valley that ran between them and the river. The boys found a good spot to bed down near the river. There were better spots near the cliffs but Gilbert expressed fear that rocks would come tumbling down from the cliffs and crush them in their sleep. They gave in to his concerns and moved closer to the river.

Pete said, "You know boys, I'm glad you chose this spot. See that house over there?" He pointed towards a two story house set in a little hollow about a mile away. "My uncle Henry lives over there. I feel bad that I didn't cart along any grub. You boys get things set up here and I'm gonna run over there and fetch us back somethin' special."

He took off running toward the house. His long, effortless strides ate up the distance quickly.

"Oh my!" exclaimed Isaac, "That feller can sure fly! Look at him go! I bet he could outrun a deer!"

The boys cleaned up some brush and gathered some wood to build a fire. By the time they had their camp site set up Pete returned. He was carrying two big earthen jugs. "Here's somethin for after supper boys. If you share with me, I'll share with you. This is the best corn liquor in the state of Ohio. It's a gift for us from Uncle Henry who says to tell you all thank you for going to defend our country. He said if he was young enough he'd come along with us."

"All right then, let's eat!" said Isaac. "Slice me off some of that ham and hand me a biscuit."

The boys wolfed down the ham and biscuits. For desert they had biscuits with either honey or raspberry jelly smeared on them.

"What about this salt pork and cornbread?" asked Isaac.

"We'll save that for breakfast in the mornin'." replied Gilbert. "We got enough of that to go around. Wonder what kind of food they gonna give us over there?"

"Pete said, "I heard you get a lot of salt pork and crackers called hard tack. Of course you can forage around for other food and buy different kinds if you have the money."

He popped the cork out of one of the jugs, took a long swig and with a grimace on his face passed it over to Isaac. "Whew! Here, this stuff will make you forget about food for a while."

Isaac took his turn and passed the jug on. It made its round several times and was soon empty. The boys were feeling pretty good when Gilbert started to sing: "Yes we'll rally round the flag boys, we'll rally once again, Shouting the battle cry of Freedom."

The others joined in and they sang that song several times as they popped open the other jug and passed it around. On both sides of the river you could see campfires dotting the shoreline. Those men were going to join the 4th also. The cool clear night air carried their voices across the river. You could hear them singing their songs as well. It seemed surreal. The clear night sky was carpeted with millions of stars. There was no breeze, the smoke from the campfire wafted straight up into the heavens.

The songs continued as Gabriel broke out in one of his favorite songs:

Get out the way, ole Dan Tucker,
You're too late to get your supper.
Supper's over and breakfast is a cookin',
Old Dan Tucker just stands there lookin'.

Wafting across the river you could hear the strains of:

Oh Susannah, don't you cry for me,
For I'm bound for Loosiana with my banjo on my knee.

Somewhere across the river a group of men were singing:

"Mine eyes have seen the coming of the Glory of the Lord,
He is trampling out the vintage where the grapes of wrath are stored.
He has loosed the fateful lightning of His terrible swift sword
His truth is marching on."

There was quiet for a moment when a group of men on the Ohio side started singing a song no one had heard before. Everyone listened as a few voices from other sites joined in this song:

When Johnny comes marching home again, Hurrah! Hurrah!
We'll give him a hearty welcome then, Hurrah! Hurrah!
The men will cheer and the boys will shout, the ladies they will all turn out
And we'll all feel gay when
Johnny comes marching home.
The old church bell will peal with joy, Hurrah! Hurrah!
To welcome home our darling boy, Hurrah! Hurrah!
The village lads and lassies say, with roses they will strew the way,
And we'll all feel gay when

Johnny comes marching home.

Get ready for the Jubilee,Hurrah! Hurrah!
We'll give the hero three times three,Hurrah!
Hurrah!
The laurel wreath is ready now to place upon his
loyal brow
And we'll all feel gay when
Johnny comes marching home.

Let love and friendship on that day,Hurrah, hurrah!
Their choicest pleasures then display,Hurrah,
hurrah!
And let each one perform some part, to fill with joy
the warrior's heart,
And we'll all feel gay when
Johnny comes marching home.

These refrains were repeated several times and soon every group of men along the river was singing it. The sound of their singing grew very loud for a quite while then began to fade as one by one, the singers began retiring for the night. At last one lone, solitary voice could be heard singing, "And we'll all feel gay when Johnny comes marching home."

Somewhere from upriver, a person yelled, "Shut up, it's time to go to sleep!"

Off in the distance you could hear a coonhound baying at the silence. Gabriel spread his blanket on the ground. He laid himself along the edge and pulled the other side up over him. As he stared at the stars twinkling in the heavens his thoughts soon turned to Lorena and he wondered what she was doing just then.

Back in Letart, Lorena had just gone to bed. She held the pendant up to her face, kissed it and gazing at its beauty, she thought of Gabriel.

Chapter XIII
Reporting for Duty / July 22, 1861

The boys began to wake up as the sun began to crest over the eastern hills along the river. James said," Come on boys, let's get rousted up and get on down to the ferry".

One by one, they got up, folded their blankets then went down to the river's edge to wash the sleep from their eyes. Gabriel was the last one to roll out of his blanket. He hadn't slept much that night. His thoughts were filled with Lorena.

Mark stirred the dying embers of their fire and added some more wood. He soon had a good fire going. "Wished we'd had brought some coffee."

"Never even thought about it." said Isaac, "How about you Pete, you got any?"

"No sir, never crossed my mind either."

"Well, let's eat up that salt pork and corn bread then head on down to the ferry."

The boys gobbled down their breakfast and walked back up towards the road as the sun breached the horizon and cast its warm rays over the countryside. There was a hint of a breeze beginning to blow.

"Looks like it's gonna be a hot one today!' said Gabriel. "Hope we get some rain to cool things down a bit."

They had walked but a short ways when a man with a team of horses and a large empty wagon came up behind them. He stopped his team and asked, "Where you boys headed fer?"

"The ferry." answered James, "We're goin across the river to get mustered in with the 4th West Virginia Infantry."

"If you boys want to ride, hop in back there, I'm headin' for Middleport myself to pick up some supplies. I'll be goin right past the ferry landing."

"Thank you sir!" said Gabriel as he and the men threw their baggage in the wagon and started climbing in. "It sure is gonna be a hot one today isn't it? We're might glad to ride with you."

After the boys introduced themselves, the old man said, "Pleased to meet you boys, my name is McBride. Got me a small farm along the river near Syracuse, almost to Minersville. I'm gonna give up farmin' though. Bought me a general store there in Syracuse. Headin' for Middleport to finalize the sale and pick up some merchandise."

"Had me a brother-in-law who had a store over in Phillipi, Virginia. Got kilt there by them stinkin' Rebs last month when they tried to take the railroad. My sister will be comin back to live with me and my wife soon as she can sell the store there."

Gabriel moved to the back corner of the wagon. He sat down and rested his back against the side. He put his elbow on top of the wagon gate and rested his head in the palm of his hand. Isaac Adams was sitting in the other corner doing the same thing.

Although the ride was bumpy, Gabriel somehow managed to doze off. He began to dream about his Lorena. In his mind he was sitting with her in the swing on her father's front porch. He had his arm around her shoulders. She placed her hand behind his head and pulled him towards her. As their cheeks brushed against each other, he could smell the lavender perfume she was wearing and as he deeply kissed her, he could taste her sweetness. His hand went up to cup her breast and just as it got there, the chain holding the swing to the porch ceiling gave way and they went tumbling off the back of the porch. When he hit the ground, he couldn't stand up.

In actuality, the wagon had run over a large rock in the road and the huge jolt, knocked open the latch that was holding the wagon gate up. As a result, the gate fell and Gabriel tumbled out of the back of the wagon and onto the dusty road where he rolled as he hit the ground.

When he finally stopped rolling, he heard the laughter of the men in the wagon. He jumped up with clinched fists and yelled, "What in the hell are you a laughin' for, I could'a been killed!"

This brought on another, louder round of laughter as the men pointed at Gabriel. To his embarrassment, he looked down and noticed the bulge in his pants. He quickly covered it up with his hands and turned his back towards his tormentors.

"We know what you was dreamin' about Gabe." Mark said, "You was mumblin' to Isaac there about how much you loved him when the gate fell down and you went tumblin' out the back!"

"I don't care how much you love me!" yelled Isaac jokingly, "I ain't a marryin' you nohow, I've already been spoke for!"

This brought on another round of laughter as Gabe sheepishly climbed back into the wagon. Mr. McBride re-latched the gate and told Gabe to move on up a little closer towards the front.

As Mr. McBride pulled his team to a stop at the ferry landing, the boys climbed out of the wagon and thanked him for the ride.

"Good luck boys, it's a pleasure knowin' you. Me and the missus will remember you all in our prayers."

They walked down the cobblestone ramp to the ferryboat and James asked the ferryman how much to carry them across the river.

"You boy's goin over to join the 4th?"

"Yes sir."

"Then you don't have to pay me nuthin'. As long as you boys are in the service of our country, you ride for free on my boat. C'mon aboard, gettin' ready to cast off now."

The ferryboat had a large wooden paddle wheel mounted on the side. This wheel was driven by a steam engine whose fire was stoked with coal. The black smoke belched out of its one smokestack as it moved slowly over the river with its nose pointed slightly upstream to avoid being carried away from the landing on the other side by the river's swift current.

"Seems like we're hardly movin' at all when you look up or down the river" James said, "but when you look at the shoreline goin' away, you can tell we're movin' pretty fast."

When they reached the other side, the ferryman dropped the loading ramp and told the boys, "Just head up river from here towards Mason City. It's about a mile or two to the camp. You can see it from the road. Good luck boys."

They each thanked the ferryman, shouldered their gear and started their trek to the camp. After a couple miles of dusty walking, the boys saw the camp off to their right. There were three huge white tents surrounded by many, many smaller ones. There were people walking around everywhere, more people in one place that any of them had ever seen before. Some dressed in Yankee blue uniforms, some in regular clothes like those that they were wearing.

They walked up to a uniformed man and asked him if he knew where they were supposed to go to be mustered in. He directed them to one of the huge white tents.

As they approached the tent, a soldier wearing the stripes of a corporal stopped them and asked, "What company do you men belong to?"

"Company E," replied James.

"Then go over there under that big tree with the rest of those men and wait until someone comes to get you."

"Yes sir", said Mark.

"Don't call me sir; I am a Corporal, Corporal Bennett. I ain't no officer. I work for my livin'! Now get over there."

"Yes Corporal."

They went over to the tree and joined about 30 other men sitting in the shade.

"What in the world is goin' on here? Just look at all them people scurryin' around like a bunch of chickens chasin' a June bug."

"Why do they keep bangin' those damn drums over there? It's givin' me a headache!"

"Them boys are gonna be drummer boys. My little brother's one. They's a teachin' them how to drum commands so's when we're in a fight, we'll know what direction to go and what to do."

Some complained of being thirsty and soon buckets of water with tin ladles were brought over and they all had a cool drink, which was a welcome relief. The air was scorching. Shimmering heat waves could be seen rising from the tops of the white tents. The air was stagnant and hardly any breeze at all. Even sitting in the shade of that tree, they were drenched with sweat. Old Glory hung limply atop the flagpole in front of the main tent.

Corporal Bennett came over and told the men to leave all their gear under the tree, form a single line and follow him.

"I'm takin' you men over to get mustered in. When we get to the tent, you will stop and enter one at a time. The adjutant will ask you your name, where you're from and what kind of work you've done. When he's finished with you, you will return to this staging area and wait."

It took almost two hours for all the men to be mustered in. Then they sat in the shade of the tree for another hour before an officer came over and told them all to stand up.

"Gentlemen, I am 2nd Lieutenant Cooper. I will be in charge of your first few days of training. First, I want to welcome you as fellow soldiers of the 4th Infantry. Your country and your president thank you for your service."

"Gentlemen, you are about to begin your training to become warriors. You will learn the proper techniques of battle. You will learn military discipline. You will learn to obey the commands of your superiors and respect their rank. All officers will be addressed as "Sir". Non-commissioned officers will be addressed by their rank. Most of our non-commissioned officers are veterans of the Mexican War. It would behoove you to listen to what they tell you. They are experienced soldiers and what you learn from them may save your life one day."

"Starting tomorrow morning you will be issued uniforms and equipment. It is your responsibility to keep your uniforms clean and respectable. It is your responsibility to maintain all of the equipment issued to you."

"There will be no alcohol allowed on the grounds. There will be no women allowed to enter the grounds. You will be expected to obey all camp rules. If not, proper punishment will be meted out."

"You will be required to follow the chain of command if you have a grievance or a request. The chain of command is as follows: Your non commissioned officers: Corporal, Sergeant, First Sergeant, and Sergeant Major. Your commissioned officers: 2nd Lieutenant, 1st Lieutenant, Captain, Major, Lieutenant Colonel, Colonel, Brigadier General, Major General, and Lieutenant General."

"Company E has been sequestered in the northeast quadrant of the camp. There is a small creek running just behind your camp. This creek is for drinking water only. Do not use it for bathing, washing your clothes or relieving yourselves. This water must remain pure. You can go down to the river for your bathing and clothes washing. Anyone caught using the creek for purposes other than drinking water will be severely punished."

"Corporal Bennett will now take you to your camp. There are tents already set up. Each tent will hold four men. Stow your gear and report to the mess area for rations. If you have any questions, rest assured they will be answered once your training begins. Corporal Bennett, you may now take over."

"Men, when I give the command "Fall In" I want you to pick up your gear and line up four abreast. My next command will be "Forward March" and you will keep the formation and follow me."

"Fall in!"

The men gathered up their belongings and shuffled into formation.

"Forward, Harch!"

They began their walk to their campsite. Upon arrival Corporal Bennett yelled, "Company, Halt."

Some of the men bumped into the men in front of them and some words were exchanged.

"All right fellers, fall out, choose your tents and stow your gear. I'll be back for you in a while to take you to the mess area to get some supper."

After the men ate their supper, which gave them their first taste of hardtack, they returned to their tents and were advised by Corporal Bennett to retire early.

"Your day tomorrow begins at sunup and it will be a long, hot, hard one. Git all the rest you can."

The boys decided to walk down to the river to swim before retiring. Many of the others joined them. The cool water of the Ohio refreshed them and raised their spirits. The evening air was filled with their laughter. They returned to their tents and after a short period of meeting and introducing themselves to each other, they crawled into their tents and went to sleep.

As soon as the morning sun breached the hills, the cool morning air was filled with the sounds of bugles blaring and corporals shouting to wake up the men.

The men of Company E were formed into ranks and marched to another huge tent where they were to receive their uniforms. They were each issued a Yankee blue jacket that sported brass buttons, 2 pair of blue trousers with a narrow white stripe down each leg, and 2 white undershirts made of cotton with long sleeves, two pairs of socks a hat and a pair of canvass leggings. They each received one belt of black dyed leather and a brass belt buckle emblazoned with the letters U.S.A. The shoes issued to them were square toed with ankle high tops. They were made of leather dyed black.

The men were instructed to return to their tents and put on their uniforms with the exception of their jackets. They were instructed to swap with each other if needed to obtain the correct sizes. They were given two hours to accomplish this, report to the mess area for breakfast and return to the supply tent.

Once they reported back to the supply tent, they were issued the following items: Each received a rifle, which was a modified 1841 U.S. Army rifle. They had all been re-bored from .54 to .58 caliber and equipped to support a stud fitted sword bayonet. They also received a cartridge box with 40 rounds, a cap pouch, a haversack, a knapsack, a canteen, a tin cup and plate, a blanket, a gum rain poncho and a shelter half.

The men were now fully equipped and their introduction to army and camp life began. Each day started at sunrise with reveille, roll call and sometimes a drill. Shortly after roll call came breakfast, followed by sick call and then a general cleaning up of the company streets.

Guard mounting then followed. This was when the First Sergeant turned out his detail for the next twenty-four hours of picket duty.

The next call was for drill, which usually lasted until around noon. The men were permitted about an hour to eat. This was followed by another period of more drill until the late afternoon. The companies were then dismissed.

From this time until reveille the next morning, the men were pretty much left on their own. They occupied their free time by reading, playing cards, and writing letters.

Several men had brought along banjos, fiddles, guitars and flutes. Sometimes there would be gatherings of these men and the air would soon be filled with the voices of the men singing numerous songs accompanied by their instruments.

Sometimes the men would play Townball or pitch horseshoes for recreation. Often a few would sneak out of camp, go into Mason City, and buy corn liquor. Several were caught and the punishment was being bucked and gagged or being forced to carry a heavy log around all day. This was followed by extended picket duty.

One night after a long day of endless drilling and fatigue duty, the men gathered around the fire to drink some coffee. Isaac Adams said, "This here army life's not what I thought it was gonna be. Hell, I thought we'd be given uniforms and a rifle, go shoot some Rebs then go back home! I can't see why they's a makin us do all this marchin' and tossin' our rifles around." He rubbed his arm and continued, "Here all my life, I thought these were called arms. Now all I hear is 'em bein' called "harms". You know, "Right Shoulder Harms! Left Shoulder Harms! Order Harms! And those damn Harchin' orders, Forward Harch! Column Right, Harch. Right Oblique, Harch. Just what in the hell is a Harch anyway?"

His brother Mark added, "When they gonna let us go fight? We ain't doin any good runnin' around here. They need to get us into the fight so's we can get this war over with and go home."

Corporal Bennet happened to be nearby and overheard the brothers talking. He walked over to their fire knelt down and said, "Boys, I know you are all anxious to take on the Rebs and you think all this bullshit you are going through here is meaningless. Let me tell you, when you get into a major fight with the enemy, all the trainin' you are receivin' now will be invaluable. Discipline and the ability to follow orders regardless of how nonessential they seem to you now will mean everything to you then. I was at Palo Alto in 48 and let me tell you, I was certainly glad for the little trainin' I had."

"In battle boys, chaos and terror are the rulin' factors. Without discipline and the knowledge you are gainin' here, the battle would be lost before it began. The first time a shell burst nearby, half of these men would be runnin' in the other direction. So you just knuckle down and learn everythin' you can. It could save your life some day. Good night boys."

They watched him walk away towards another group of men. James said, "You know, what the Corporal said makes sense. I've been thinkin' about what it could be like."

"What do you mean?" asked Gabriel.

"You know, bein' in a battle and havin' to kill someone. It's easy to talk about, but what's it like to actually have to take another man's life?" I know Papaw went through it, I wish I could have talked to him more about his war experience."

Isaac said, "Hell James, all you gotta do is point your rifle at 'em and pull the trigger! That ain't too hard."

"Killin' from a distance is one thing" said Mark, "but what if the fightin' is close, hand to hand. Could you run your bayonet through the belly of a man, would you be able to do that like we do those sacks of straw we been trainin' on?"

"Hell yeah, replied Isaac, "Especially if he's tryin' to run his bayonet through my belly!"

Pete stood up and towering above the others said, "I know where the Corporal is coming from, when he was talking about discipline and training. They are conditioning us so we will be able to do whatever is necessary to win the fight. Just like a racehorse is conditioned to win a race. We must know when to react and when not to react in different situations; we must know how to fight in certain conditions and circumstances. If they had just given us a rifle and said, "Go get 'em boys!" We'd all probably be dead right now."

Isaac, who was lying on his side by the fire looked up at Pete and said, "Petey, I gotta a question for you, answer me truly for I'd really like to know one thing."

"What's that?" asked Pete.

"Promise me you'll tell the truth?"

"I will!" said Pete, "Now, what's the question?"

"Do you ever get nose bleeds bein up there so far?"

Pete responded with a kick to Isaac's backside, which brought a round of laughter.

"I'm going to bed" he said, "I'll see you fellers in the mornin'."

"Tell me a story Petey," whined Isaac, "so's I can go to sleep!"

Pete stopped, turned and said, "Go fuck a duck!"

This brought on another round of laughter as the men got up and prepared to retire for the evening.

Chapter XIV
Point Pleasant / Gallipolis / Papaw's condition worsens

Around the first week of August, Colonel Lightburn, their commanding officer, received orders to move the 4th to Point Pleasant. Some of the companies made the march and others were boarded on steamers at Mason City.

At Point Pleasant, the men began to learn military tactics and continued to drill and perform the manual of arms. They carved their names on the back of their belt buckles. An old soldier, a veteran of the Mexican War told them to do this.

"In case you're killed and no one knows who you are." The old soldier said. "Sometimes there's not much left of a body to identify after a big fight."

Gabriel carved "Gabriel Wheeler, Letart Falls, O and Arcadia.

Passes were issued to the men so they could visit the town of Point Pleasant or cross the river to Gallipolis to spend some of their first pay.

The Wheeler brothers and Danny chose to take the ferry across to Gallipolis. There they posted some letters and bought some onions and potatoes. The rations the army issued were Salt pork, beef, ham or bacon, hardtack or soft bread, rice and beans, desiccated vegetables, dried apples and peaches and coffee, tea, sugar salt, pepper and molasses. They were craving onions, some of the men used ramps to add to their diet, but they were more like garlic. The boys were craving some of the big white onions like they used to raise on their farm at Letart Falls. They were fortunate to find some from a farmer outside of Gallipolis. He also had some of the Ohio River

Potatoes that they loved so well. They bought a sack of yams from him also and headed back to camp.

Gabriel had written to Lorena every other day and needed to replenish his supply of 3-cent coins. James and Mark had also gotten some from the bank in Gallipolis. Lorena had written often also. Mail was sometimes slow though and un-regular. Sometimes he would receive two or three letters at a time. Each had been written on different days.

In his letters, Gabriel would tell Lorena how much he missed her and loved her. He would describe camp life and how boring it was. He would occasionally write a page or two to his parents as would Mark and they would include them with the letters James would send to their parents.

Lorena's letters would be filled with her love and descriptions of events at Arcadia. She told him how she enlisted the help of Erissa and her two boys to help keep it beautiful. They had planted more flowers and cleared out a bigger area right up to the meadow.

In the last letter, she told him how she would gaze at the pendant and know that Gabriel was thinking of her at the same time. "Gabe, I couldn't sleep last night so I walked down to Arcadia. The moon was so bright. I sat down on our rock and was gazing up at the sky. I swear Gabe, I could hear your voice in the breezes as they blew through the trees. You were telling me that someday you would join me here at Arcadia and not to cry. I felt so comforted by that. I laid the pendant on the rock, got undressed and dove into the water. As the darkness of the water closed over my head, there was silence. When I surfaced, I swear I could hear your laughter. I miss you so much."

Gabe looked at the date on the letter. He remembered that night. It was so bright out. He couldn't sleep either and had taken a walk down to the river. As he stood there gazing across the moving water, his thoughts were filled with Lorena. He closed his eyes. He could picture her sitting on the rock crying. He said aloud, "Lorena, Lorena, Don't cry, I'll be there with you soon." As he turned to walk back to camp, he remembered the time he first kissed Lorena and he laughed as he remembered the look of surprise in her eyes.

Lorena only removed the pendant from her neck when she bathed or swam at Arcadia. She would clutch it whenever she thought of Gabriel and that was often.

She visited the Wheeler house almost every day and talked with John and Elva, they would let her read the letters they got from the boys and she would read parts of the letters she got from Gabriel to them. Erissa would read parts of Mark's letters and they would all say a little prayer.

Papaw Isaac was getting worse in his senility. More often that not, he stayed in bed only to get up to eat or relieve himself. On occasion when he would wander outside, John or Elva would have to lead him back into the house. He would protest that he had work to do and wanted to know where the boys were.

They had to make sure the door was locked at night for Isaac would sometimes get up and wander out into the meadow or down the road towards the McPhersons.

He would talk to himself and make statements that made no sense. It was as if he was communicating with people around him that no one else could see.

One night John heard his father talking in the kitchen. He got out of bed to check on him. As he entered the kitchen he said, "Pa! Are you all right?"

Isaac was sitting at the table cleaning his pistol in the dark. Startled he turned and said, "Cap, Cap, did you see any injuns out there?

"It's me! John! There ain't no injuns out there Pa,"

"John? Hell, I thought you was Cap. There's a heavy fog formin' tonight. Make sure you keep your powder dry. There's gonna be hell to pay in the mornin'. Them injuns have been screamin' and poundin' their drums all night. Cap, you better melt your extra lead and make all the balls you can. We're gonna need 'em tomorrow."

"Pa! Pa! It's me, John, your son!"

John lit a candle and sat down next to his father. "Cap ain't here Pa, he's been dead for over 40 years and there ain't no injuns around here anymore! Why don't you let me get you a glass of cider then you can go on back to bed and get some rest."

Isaac squinted his eyes, looked at John and then he gazed down at his pistol.

John got up and poured two glasses of cider. "Here Pa, drink this." Isaac took the glass and drained it in one gulp.

"Where's my boys John? Why are you keepin' them from me? I ain't seen 'em for so long. Where's my little Gabriel?"

"They ain't boys no more Pa, they've all grown up. They're young men now and they're all away fightin' for their country just like you done Pa. They'll be comin' home soon."

"John, John, let's me and you go fetch 'em back now afore they get hurt or kilt."

"We can't do that Pa. It wouldn't be right and besides you're in no shape to travel."

"I know son. Sometimes I don't know whether I'm a comin' or a goin'. These old legs of mine don't seem to want to go where I want 'em to. Oh, how wish I was young again sometimes and with my sweet Sissy. I miss her so much. If I'd a knowed that she and the boys wouldn't be there when I got back I never would have went off with Cap to fight. If only, there was a way for one to go back in time and do things different.

Those few years I spent with Sissy were some of the happiest times of my life."

"Come on Pa; let's get you back to bed. You'll feel better in the mornin'."

Isaac went willingly with John gently guiding him by his arm. As the old man lay down, he looked up and said. "Thank you Cap,"

The next morning, John was telling Elva about this incident. She said, "John, do you remember that Chapman fellow who stayed with us for a while, a long time ago? You know the one who sold us those apple trees."

"Yes, I remember him, he was quite a fellow. I wonder whatever happened to him."

Elva continued, "Anyway, I was talkin' to him once about Heaven and he said that most people have a misconception of Heaven and what it really is. He said most people think you spend the entire time flyin' around, playin' harps and singin' songs. He said that the way he figures it, Heaven is a place where whatever made you happy in this life, you will experience again. Only this time with no sadness involved."

"He said, "There is no sorrow in Heaven, the Bible says so. Therefore, if there is no sorrow, then all the bad things that happened to you in this life won't happen to you again."

"Your Pa will be with your Ma again and this time no sickness or death can ever separate them."

"In other words, Heaven will be just like livin' your life here but without all the things that can cause sadness. There'll be no death, no sickness, no war, and no separation from your loved ones."

"He said it is hard to understand because we as humans always try to figure things out in the physical sense rather than the spiritual. He said after a person dies, everythin' is spiritual and your existence has no boundaries, no limitations and time is eternal. That

John Chapman was a smart man. I've often thought about this as he made Heaven sound like such a beautiful place to spend eternity."

"He sure was a smart fellow," said John, and he seemed to know what he was talkin' about."

Chapter XV

Isaac the Prankster / Papaw's Death /

Isaac Adams was a prankster and he loved to tease the gentle giant Pete. It was a well-known fact that Pete had a deathly fear of any kind of snake. Whenever they were on patrol and someone shouted snake, Isaac noticed Pete always changed directions he was walking so he moved away from the area. Whenever they bivouacked, Pete would spend a lot of time looking around before he laid out his blanket to sleep.

One day, while out on patrol, Corporal Bennet had the men stop to eat their hard tack and take a break. After looking around, Pete sat down and leaned his back up against a tree. It wasn't long before he was in a sound sleep.

Isaac couldn't resist the opportunity to play a prank on his tall friend. He had found a dead blacksnake that morning and stuffed all five feet of it into his knapsack. He got down on his belly and crawled up to Pete's feet. He very carefully untied Pete's shoelaces and then tied them together.

He then crawled back to his knapsack and took out the snake. He carefully and quietly made his way behind the tree that Pete was leaning against. Reaching around, he laid the dead snake across Pete's lap. He then took a long switch and began poking Pete's thigh.

Pete abruptly awoke, saw the snake and went berserk. He let out a horrific scream. He jumped up, knocking the snake to the ground and tried to take off running. His feet never caught up with the top part of his body because of his shoelaces being tied together. He went tumbling head over heels.

Of course, Isaac couldn't restrain himself. He rolled on the ground laughing so hard he couldn't stand up.

Once Pete realized that his little friend was involved, his fear turned to anger. He quickly retied his shoelaces, went over and picked Isaac up off the ground by his belt and shirt collar. He carried him over to a nearby creek and slung his little friend out as far as he could.

Isaac came up sputtering and coughing. "Aw Petey, you ain't mad are ya? I was just havin' a little fun. I thought I could help you get over bein' so scared of snakes."

"Pete pointed his finger at Isaac and warned. "If you ever put another snake on me I swear, I will stuff him up your nose, every inch of it!"

Pete tried to get his revenge a couple days later.

"Isaac, try some of this sassafras tea I made. It's good and cold, used water from a spring."

He handed Isaac a lidded pewter drinking cup filled with the tea and in which he had placed a small, four-inch live garter snake. Isaac took the cup, thumbed open the lid and began to drink. The little snake went right into his mouth.

He paused drinking, reached into his mouth and pulled out the little garter snake. He looked up at Pete who was laughing at him. He put the wriggling snake back in his mouth, chewed it up and swallowed it. He then washed it down with what was left of the sassafras tea. He handed the cup back to Pete.

"Thank you for that fine tea and the little snack you included with it, what's for dessert?"

Pete couldn't believe what he'd just seen. His stomach churned and he hurriedly went over behind his tent and threw up.

Isaac sat there laughing at his big friend as he reached into his mouth, pulled the still wriggling garter snake out, and tossed him into the brush.

October 1, 1861

This morning, long before the roosters began to crow, the men were awakened by the sound of the drummer boys beating a call to roll. Corporal Bennett and Sergeant Myers were running up the camp street yelling for everyone to "get up, get dressed and fall in!"

Roll call was taken and after a hasty breakfast, the men were ordered to prepare to leave this place. Four companies, including Company E, were ordered to march to Point Pleasant and board steamers where they were soon headed up the Kanawha River.

The men disembarked at the mouth of the Pocatalico River. They marched about eight miles up that river where they were ordered to bivouac. It was a long, tiring walk. The men were carrying almost all of their gear. They had to cross several creeks and streams. They were soaked and tired to the bone when they finally stopped to bivouac.

That evening the Wheeler brothers and Danny McPherson walked down to the river to fill their canteens. They were just finishing when a large meteor sizzled across the night sky and lit up the whole area. It disappeared behind some hills and the boys anticipated an explosion for they thought sure it was going to strike the ground. None came, just an eerie silence as the boys gazed up into the heavens. "Papaw!" thought Gabriel.

The next morning the men were marched to a little town named Spencer, in Roane County. They had been told they were going there to relieve the Home Guard who was defending the place from Rebel bushwhackers. The Rebs had been besieging the town for several days. Just before they arrived, the Home Guard had succeeded in driving the Confederate forces away.

The men set up camp and awaited further orders. During the first week, provisions were scarce. Mark had found a farmer who agreed to sell him some green corn and a few potatoes. The farmer said that "Those damn Rebel bushwhackers" had already stolen most of his produce! He had got a few shots off at some of them the other night. "Thought I'd wounded one as he fell off his horse when I shot, but could find no blood the next morning."

After ten days, a train arrived at Spencer with provisions and the mail. In the mail was a letter from home addressed to James.

October 5, 1861

Dear James, Mark, Gabriel and Danny,

I have some bad news for you boys. Your Papaw Isaac has passed away. Boys don't be too sad. We all know his soul is in a better place now. His condition had been getting worse and worse. We could hardly talk to him. Towards the end of last month, Pa scrounging around in the kitchen awakened me one night. He was mumbling, yelling, and talking to someone. I got up and as I entered the room, he looked at me and said, "Cap, Cap, have you seen my pistol? I was just a cleanin it and laid it down somewhere, now I can't find it!" I knew who Cap was. Cap was a man who your Papaw knew a long time ago. They fought in the war together. Cap was killed by Indians at the Battle of the Thames. I decided to go along with Pa and said," Isaac, I'll fetch your pistol for you. I know where you left it." I went over to the mantle, removed the charge from the pistol, and handed it to him. He took it from me and said, "I'm sure glad you found it Cap, I wouldn't go without it; my Pa gave me this here pistol told me never to let it out of my sight." He seemed at ease then and I led him back to his bed. When I got up the next morning, he was gone. Somehow, he climbed out of the window. I went looking for him but couldn't find him. I went over to the McPhersons and Ed and Lorena helped me look for him. We found him down there at the creek at Arcadia. He was floating face down in the pool there, just off the flat rock. Ed and Lorena pulled him out, as I had no strength at all. In his hand was clutched that pistol. I think he thought he was going into battle and walked or fell into the water. We buried him in the cemetery next to Maggie and the babies. Ed built the coffin and we put his pistol in there with him. We got a wooden cross up there now but when you boys get home, we'll get a proper stone marker for his grave. You boys should know that your Papaw Isaac loved each one of you and was so proud of you boys. Do him honor in battle, be brave but not foolish.

Pa

Chapter XVI
Passing Letart on the River / The Lost Bayonet

The Company received orders to rejoin the rest of the 4th. They marched to the town of Ravenswood in Jackson County and there they boarded steamers to take them down the Ohio River to Point Pleasant.

As the boats passed Letart Island, the men could see people on the shoreline waving at them. "Look! Right over there!" shouted Mark, "There's Ma and Pa!"

Isaac, Gabe and Danny, strained to make out the faces of the people standing on the shore.

"Looks like them, can't tell for sure. We're so dadburned far away! Can't see their faces" Said James.

Gabriel looked frantically for Lorena. His eyes focused on a girl and as he stared at her, the bright afternoon sun caused a brilliant red flash to appear on her chest. Gabe knew it was Lorena. It was the reflection of the sun on the red pendant. He then could make out his Ma, Pa, and Erissa.

"That's them, right there by that big rock!" he yelled. He started waving frantically.

"Look!" Shouted Mark, "Everyone's there! There's your Ma and Pa, Danny, and there's Erissa standing beside Lorena!"

"There's your boys Mark! I don't see Susan, oh, there she is! On the other side of the rock!"

They all began waving. On the shore looking out, the folks could only see a lot of men dressed in blue uniforms lining the rails of the boats. Everyone on the boats was waving. They couldn't make out who was who.

Before anyone could realize what was happening, Gabriel climbed up on top of the railing. He looked like he was going to jump into the river. Danny grabbed him and pulled him back down.

"Don't do it Gabe! They shoot deserters!"

"I wasn't gonna jump, I just wanted to get up on the rail to see better!"

He climbed back up and began waving with both hands. His movement caught Lorena's eye.

"There he is!" She cried, "There's Gabe up on the rail of that big ole boat!"

She began climbing up on the big rock and when she reached the top, she stood and waved both hands. Her eyes were focused on Gabriel and his eyes were locked on her. They couldn't get her to come down off the rock until the boat was around the bend and out of sight. The same with Gabriel, his brothers had to pull him down from the rail.

When the men arrived at Point Pleasant, they were issued new uniforms, which were heartily welcomed. The march from Spencer to Ravenswood was miserable. There were heavy rains, the men were forced to march through mud, and cross streams that were so swollen that they were sometimes up to their waist in muddy water. They were also issued new winter shoes, great coats and extra blankets.

While they were at Point Pleasant, they ran into an old friend. Old Doctor Philson had been appointed Assistant Surgeon. He had the boys come over to his quarters one evening to share coffee and talk. He asked about their families and how they had been doing since becoming soldiers. He reminded them that he had brought each one of them into this world. He was sad to hear about Isaac.

"He was a good fellow," Said Doctor Philson, "not many like him. I know he was suffering from dementia and senility. I wish there was something I could have done for him."

When they were ready to leave, Doctor Philson said, "Boys, wait a minute, I have something for you."

He slowly walked into another room and could be heard shuffling boxes around. When he returned, he handed Danny a large cardboard box wrapped in paper.

"Here you boys take this with you. I hope you enjoy it."

"What is it Doc?"

"It's some kind of black walnut fruitcake that my wife made for me. She made me one before and for some reason she thinks I like it. She made me two more. I can barely stand to smell it, let alone eat it. It'll go to waste if I keep it so you boys take it and if you don't like it, chuck it in the river or give it to someone else. You boys take care of yourselves now."

The boys tried the cake, but couldn't eat it. They gave it to the Adams brothers who thought it was a delicacy and ate every bite.

Their stay at Point Pleasant was a short one. They soon got orders to proceed to Ceredo where they spent the winter and most of the following spring. There was battalion drill nearly every day and the regiment was noted for its fine appearance, noble bearing and its precise military movements.

Colonel Lightburn had ordered that no intoxicating liquors would be permitted in the camp but some of the men devised a way to checkmate the Colonel's order. They would procure a pass and go into the town of Catlettsburg, Kentucky where there was "an abundance of unadulterated juice of the corn."

After drinking all they wanted there, they would fill up the barrel of their muskets with the stuff and cork up the muzzles. They would carry it right past the guards and when they got back to camp would sell it or give it to their friends.

Isaac lost his bayonet, or else it was stolen. He could not find it anywhere or one to replace it. Colonel

Lightburn himself was to inspect the troops tomorrow morning and he had to have one for inspection. Isaac was desperate with worry. All offers made to buy one from other soldiers were turned down. He could not make himself steal one.

Pete told Isaac to use his head. "Carve you one out of wood and stain it black. You can use my bayonet as a model. You still have your sheath so all you need is something to put in it that looks like a bayonet then hope you're not asked to produce it at inspection tomorrow."

Isaac went out into the woods and found a suitable piece of wood to carve. He worked on it for three or four hours and finally got it looking pretty close to the real thing. He stained the handle with leather dye and after it dried, he placed it in his sheath.

"Tolerable close" said Pete. "It should work."

The next morning the men were ordered to fall in for inspection. Colonel Lightburn moved through the lines of men at a rather quick pace so Isaac thought to himself. "He'll walk right past me, thank goodness!"

When the Colonel reached the line of men in which Isaac was standing, he ordered the first man to hand him his musket. He looked over the musket and gave it back to the soldier. He moved to the next soldier and asked for his knapsack. The soldier removed it and handed it to the Colonel who look through it and handed it back. The next soldier was Isaac. The Colonel barked, "Let me see your bayonet soldier!"

"Sir" Isaac said, "Wouldn't you rather inspect my cartridge belt or my canteen?"

"Soldier, give me your bayonet!" demanded the Colonel. "Why are you hesitating?"

"Sir", I promised my father before I left home that I would not unsheathe my bayonet unless I intended to kill with it."

"Soldier, unsheathe your bayonet now and hand it to me!"

As he was taking it out Isaac paused, looked skyward and said, "May the Lord change this bayonet to wood for breakin' my vow to my father."

Pete and the others could hardly keep from laughing. The Colonel also tried to hide a smile as Isaac handed him his wooden bayonet.

"Sergeant!" barked the Captain, "Put this man on report."

The Colonel turned and said, "Belay that order Sergeant!"

"Captain, this man obviously has direct ties to God. We'll not punish him for making him break his vow. We may need him some day to call upon the Lord to help us."

Smiling, the Colonel returned the wooden bayonet to Isaac and moved on to the next soldier.

Chapter XVII
The Song "Lorena"

Grandpa paused in his storytelling and looked up at the ceiling and at the windows. "Is this storm ever going to let up? I have never in my life seen it rain so long and so hard. Do you all want me to go on or do you want to go to bed."

"Go on Dad!" said Amy, "It's still early. We want to hear more."

Everyone chimed in saying that they wanted the old man to continue.

"All right he said, but first I have to go to the bathroom and if anyone else needs to go, now's the time."

As he got up and made his way to the bathroom, Kelli said, "Isn't it wonderful to hear Dad talking like this again? I believe it is good for him to do this. He has been so withdrawn since his stroke. This has got to be good therapy for him."

"And us too!" Casey said. "He's giving us a look into our family history here. I find it most fascinating."

Another loud crack of thunder shook the windows as the old man returned. "Better throw some more wood on the fire," he said as he sat down in his chair.

Casey and John tossed a few more logs on and Grandpa said, "Now where was I?"

"Sneakin booze into the camp and wooden bayonets!" said one of the little ones.

One cold December night, right after the men retired, Isaac got up and disappeared. His brother Gilbert noticed him leave the tent and figured he was just going outside to relieve himself. After about an hour when he didn't return, Gilbert woke up Pete and Thomas.

"Isaac's left boys and I'm worried. He's been sayin' he's sick and tired of army life. I hope he didn't skedaddle. What should we do?"

"Let's check to see if he's over in Mark and James' tent." Thomas suggested.

They went over and entered the tent. Gilbert stepped on Gabriel's hand and went sprawling when Gabe yelped in pain.

"What the hell is goin' on?" asked James.

"We're lookin for Isaac. He may have deserted." Pete answered. "Have any of you seen him?"

"No get in here and close those damn flaps. You're lettin' all the heat out! It's colder than a witch's tit outside!"

"Isaac ain't that stupid is he; to go off in cold weather like this?"

I don't know," said Gilbert, "He's been sayin' he's fed up with army life. If he puts his mind to somethin..."

"Hey, what're you fellas all doin over here?" It was Isaac. He poked his head in the tent. "Nobody was in the tent. I thought you guys had skedaddled or somethin."

"Where you been" asked Gilbert? We thought you done hightailed it."

"Hell no, I ain't no deserter. I just thought we could all use a little extra sleepin' time in the mornin' so I paid a visit to the bugler's tent. I hate to hear that damn trumpet goin off in the mornin' so I fixed it."

"What do you mean you fixed it?" Gabriel asked.

"I put a cork plug in the mouthpiece and filled that damn thing up with water. I set it outside the bugler's tent. When he gets up in the mornin', it'll be froze solid. He won't be able to toot that damn thing until he thaws it out. That way we'll all get to sleep in."

"You moron!" shouted Pete. "You kept us up half the night worryin' about you. We ain't gonna gain any more sleep!"

"Yeah, I guess you're right Petey boy, but I sure had fun doin' it and we'll all get a couple laughs in the mornin' when that sucker tries to blow his horn."

May 1, 1862

"Gabe, you're gonna have to get rid of some of those letters. If we have to go on a long march, what're you gonna do? Cart 'em all over the place?"

"Aw James, I can't bear the thought of gettin' rid of anything that Lorena created. I know they're gonna be a burden but I'm willin' to carry them."

"Gabe", said Mark, "I was talkin' to Doc Philson the other day and he said he's got leave to go back home tomorrow. Why don't you bundle them up, give them to Doc, and ask him to carry them to Lorena to keep for you. I'm sure he would do that for you, wouldn't hurt to ask."

"Here, said Danny as he tossed an empty flour sack to Gabriel, "Bundle 'em up, put 'em in here and take 'em over to Doctor Philson. He's an honorable man and he won't read any of 'em."

Gabriel gave in to his brothers and took the letters to Doctor Philson who agreed to take them to Lorena for him. "I've heard a lot about you and that McPherson girl," said Doctor Philson, "I even know about your Arcadia. A lot of people do. You got yourself a fine woman there Gabriel, and a good place to settle down. Everyone up Letart way says you and her were born for each other and I believe them. Some day, I hope to bring your children into the world. I wish, this damn war would end soon so people like you and Lorena can get your lives and families started."

Gabriel thanked the doctor and wished him a safe and enjoyable trip home.

That evening, around dusk, Gabriel walked down to the Ohio River. He was standing in silence, gazing out over the rippling waters thinking about his Lorena. Mark came down to find him. "Gabe! Gabe! Come up here!"

Concerned that there might be trouble, Gabe started up the bank in a rush and shouted, "What's wrong!"

"Nothin's wrong, I want you to come with me, you gotta hear this."

"Hear what?"

"A song, a song these fellers were singin' over by where the 9th is camped. It's a song about Lorena!"

"What?" asked Gabe, "How'd they know about Lorena?"

"Just com'on Gabe, they're waitin' on us. I asked them to sing it again for you once I got you over there."

They made their way through the camp to where the Muleskinners for the 9th had set up. There were about a dozen men sitting around a fire singing softly. There was a fiddle player, a banjo player and a soldier with a guitar sitting on barrels and bales of hay.

Mark and Gabe sat down on the ground close to the fire and when the men finished singing their song, Mark stood up and said, "Fellers, this here is my brother Gabe. He's gonna marry his childhood sweetheart and her name is Lorena, just like in that song you sung a while ago. I sure would appreciate it if you would sing it again for him."

"We'd be glad to do that for you soldier." Said the guitar player. "Pat, come up here and sing the words."

A young, blond haired soldier stood up and walked over to Gabe. He held out his hand and said, "I'm Patrick O'Ryan, my friends call me Pat and I'm pleased to meet you Gabe."

After he shook hands with Gabe, he went over and sat down on a bale of hay, next to the guitar player. The guitar player began strumming softly and was soon joined by the others. Pat, in a clear, tenor voice started to sing these words:

The years creep slowly by, Lorena,
The snow is on the grass again;
The sun's low down the sky, Lorena,
The frost gleams where the flowers have been;
But the heart throbs on as warmly now,
As when the summer days were nigh;
Oh! the sun can never dip so low,
Down affection's cloudless sky.

A hundred months have passed, Lorena,
Since last I held thy hand in mine;
And felt the pulse beat fast, Lorena --
Though mine beat faster far than thine;
A hundred months -- 'twas flowery May,
When up the hilly slope we climbed,
To watch the dying of the day,
And hear the distant church bells chime.

We loved each other then, Lorena.
More than we ever dared to tell;
And what we might have been, Lorena,
Had but our lovings prospered well --
But then -- 'tis past; the years are gone,
I'll not call up their shadowy forms;
I'll say to them, "lost years, sleep on!
Sleep on! Nor heed life's pelting storms."

The story of that past, Lorena,
Alas! I care not to repeat;
They touched some tender chords, Lorena,
They lived, but only lived to cheat.
I would not cause even one regret
To rankle in your bosom now --
"For if we try we may forget,"
Were words of thine long years ago.

Yes, those were words of thine, Lorena --
They are within my memory yet --
They touched some tender chords, Lorena,
Which thrill and tremble with regret.
'Twas not the woman's heart which spoke --
Thy heart was always true to me;
A duty stern and piercing broke
The tie that linked my soul to thee.

It matters little now, Lorena,
The past is in the eternal past;
Our hearts will soon lie low, Lorena,
Life's tide is ebbing out so fast.
There is a future, oh, thank God!
Of life, this is so small a part --
'Tis dust to dust beneath the sod,
But there, up there, 'tis heart to heart.

Tears began to stream down Gabe's face and he pulled his knees up to his chest and hid his face. As he listened to Patrick sing that song in his soft tenor voice, a vision of Lorena sitting with him on the rock at Arcadia filled his mind. He missed her terribly. When Pat finished the last verse there was nothing but silence. Gabe stood up and with a shaky voice thanked the boys while trying to mask his tears.   Mark stood up, took Gabe's arm and led him away, back towards their camp.

Chapter XVIII
The Battle of Charleston

It wasn't long before the regiment got orders to move to Charleston. The country between Charleston and Chapmansville is wild and picturesque. It is intersected with narrow valleys and deep ravines surrounded by high hills. It is also home to many Rebel soldiers.

The 2nd Battle of Bull Run was being fought in the east and General Cox, who was in command of the Kanawha Valley, was ordered to head east with as many men as could be spared. He departed with eight to ten thousand men from the Kanawha Valley and met the enemy at South Mountain and Antietam.

Left to guard the Kanawha Valley was one brigade consisting of the 34th and 37th Ohio infantries the 4th and 9th West Virginia Infantries plus two companies of the 2nd West Virginia Cavalry, which were all placed under the command of Colonel Lightburn.

"I was talkin' to a Corporal from the 9th yesterday." Mark said. "His name was Donohue, Calvin Donohue, lives over in Jackson County. He has five brothers who all joined up. Not all in the 9th though. Said his uncle named Stewart, who was 55 years old, signed up and was in the 9th with him and his brother Salathiel. His Uncle Stewart got a pass to go home last month and while he was there the Jackson County Home Guard accused him of bein' a deserter. It ended up with one them Home Guards shootin' his Uncle Stewart in the back and killin' him. He wasn't even armed. He'd left his rifle at his house when he went to talk some sense into those fellers. Donohue said there was gonnato be some hell to pay after this war is over. He said the Jackson County Home Guard is nothin' but a bunch of scum suckin' riff raff and trouble makers."

Early in September 1862, Colonel Lightburn received intelligence that Confederate General Loring was moving down the valley with an army estimated to be eight to ten thousand strong.

On the 10th of September, the Confederate advance had reached Fayette where the 37th Ohio was encamped. There was some fighting and the 37th was ordered to retreat to Charleston. Colonel Lightburn brought all the companies in to Charleston and set up the 4th and 9th West Virginia regiments along and near the Elk River.

"We're gonna have a fight on our hands soon boys" said Corporal Bennett. "We've got to hold our ground."

Company E was ready for battle. They dug in along the Elk River and set up breastworks.

"Are you scared James?" Mark asked.

"Don't know if I'm scared or just excited. I wish it would get started. You know they're comin'. It just makes me nervous havin' to wait. I want to get it over with."

First Sergeant Myers approached them and said, "I need four men, you men come with me."

They followed Sgt. Myers to a supply wagon about 100 yards behind the breastworks. He reached into the wagon and pulled out four telescopes. As he handed them to the men he said, "See that big pile of rocks right on top of that mountain there across the Kanawha? I need some videttes up there. I want you boys to get up there as quickly as possible."

He then handed them two white flags with a red squares sewn in the middle. They were attached to sticks about four feet long. If you see any movement of the enemy in mass, I want you to wave these flags, then point both flags in the direction you see them movin'.

When I said in mass boys, I don't mean when you see groups of skirmishers movin' towards us. I mean if you see them forming ranks and moving for a major assault."

He then handed them a bag of rags and a can of coal oil. If you see or hear anything at night, wrap these rags around the end of a pole, soak 'em in this coal oil and light it. Wave it back and forth. We will be watchin' you from here with telescopes. You make damn sure you stay alert and watch. Take some extra rations with you, you may be there awhile."

"The Rebs may be lookin' to occupy that place too, so be alert. Challenge anybody that comes your way. If they ain't wearin' blue, and you don't know 'em, let 'em have it."

"If and when they attack our lines, get back down here as quick as you can. If you see we're gettin' overrun, take off for Ravenswood. That's where we are gonna retreat to if necessary."

He called over two privates who were standing nearby. "This is Private Rawlings and this is Private Crawford. If I feel it's necessary to pull you down off that mountain, I'll send them up for you. Don't shoot 'em. Learn their faces and voices so you'll know them if they come up for you."

"As soon as you reach the top, wave the flags as a test. Watch for our return signal, which is this large red flag. When you see us wave back, you'll know we see you all right. Don't wave your flags again until you see the enemy advancin'. Good luck men. Remember, we're countin' on you down here. Now skedaddle up there!"

They put some extra salt pork and hardtack into their haversacks as they talked to the two Privates. Then they started out at a run to the river. They climbed in an old rowboat and paddled across the Kanawha. When they reached the other side, they moved as quickly as possible up the mountain, always alert for rebel skirmishers or snipers. Danny carried the two flags.

The mountain was very steep and soon they were on all fours trying to make their way up, clawing at the ground and grabbing tree trunks and branches. Scurrying over rocks and sometimes slipping and sliding back down the mountain. It took almost two hours to reach the top and when they did, they were exhausted.

Danny stood atop the rocks and waved the flag as the others looked through their telescopes back towards the line. They saw the red flag being waved and told Danny to stop.

They had quite a view of the area. They could see up the Kanawha Valley and most of the valley formed by the Elk River.

"There they are" said James as he peered through his telescope towards the upper end of the Elk River Valley.

The other boys put their telescopes to their eyes and could see men dressed in butternut and gray walking around. They could see the smoke from their fires and the dark gray shapes of tents scattered around the area. They could see three rebel parrot guns set up in position about half a mile from the Kanawha.

Looking down on their own lines, they could see the men and their breastworks. They could see the two parrot guns and three or four howitzers set up behind their men.

"How we gonna see 'em if they move at night?" Gabe asked.

"We'll have to use our ears as well as our eyes." James replied. "Go cut us a long pole to wrap these rags on. I wonder how these boulders ever got on top of this mountain."

"Look here!" exclaimed Mark, who had been looking around the pile of boulders. "This is almost like a cave."

There were two large boulders that were sort of leaning against each other leaving a fairly large space near the ground. It was big enough to seek shelter in if a rain should come up.

"We'll take turns watchin' and listenin' throughout the night, two at a time. Two will watch while two sleep. Danny and I will take the first watch tonight for six hours. Then Mark, you and Gabe will take the next watch."

Just as he said that one of the Confederate parrot guns opened fire. Smoke belched from the end of the cannon and the boys heard the projectile screaming as it arced across the sky. They watched as it struck a barn behind their lines. Part of the barn disintegrated and the rest caught fire as the projectile exploded.

Another Confederate gun opened up and our parrot guns answered back. The artillery barrage lasted for about an hour. Men on both sides died that afternoon, but the Confederates, with the exception of a few skirmishers who engaged the men of the 4th for a while, made no advances.

After the sun went down and darkness enveloped the region, a few musket shots could be heard as the boys in the 4th took pot shots at the Rebel skirmishers in front of their positions. The Rebels answered shot for shot but no one on either side was hit.

The gunner in charge of one of the Rebel parrots told his men, "Let's give them Billy Yanks somethin' to dream about tonight boys! Let's put a couple more into 'em."

He worked the crank to lower the cannon barrel. "I'm gonna bounce this solid shot right into their works, I want a shell shot for the next one. Get 'er ready boys, set the fuse for an aerial burst. I want it to bust right over top of their heads!"

"As soon as we fire the 2nd round, we gotta limber up and move out in case they get a fix on us. We'll move on about a hundred yards over that way."

"The shell is ready, Corporal, the fuse has been set."

"Prepare for action boys! Cannoneers, take your positions!"

"Fire!"

A Cannoneer pulled the lanyard. Fire and smoke belched out of the end of the cannon as the projectile was screaming sent down the valley. It struck the ground about 50 yards in front of the breastworks then bounced directly into them sending debris and men sailing into the air.

The Union Cannoneers scrambled to their posts beside their own guns. One of the Union Gunners cried, "I saw their flash, quickly men, wheel to the left!"

The gun crew turned the wheels of the cannon so the barrel moved to the left.

"A little more!" Cried the Gunner as he gazed down the sights on the cannon. "Now back to the right just a little. There, right there!" He adjusted his sights and cranked the end of the barrel upwards.

"Prepare to fire at my command! Quickly, we got shell in here. If we get close we can knock them out before they can limber up or set another round!"

At the same instant the Union Gunner was preparing to fire, the Confederate Cannoneers were beginning to load the 2nd round. The barrel had been sponged, the round committed. The rammer was pulling his rod from the end of the cannon. The Gunner just finished setting his sights for an airburst. One of the Cannoneers was holding the lanyard waiting for the command to fire.

The Union Gunner yelled "Fire!" The Cannoneer jerked the lanyard back and the cannon belched flame and smoke as their projectile went sailing through the night air towards the Rebel Cannon.

The Rebel Gunner was just mouthing the word "Fire!" when the Union shell hit and burst just under the Rebel cannon. The explosion tore the Rebel cannon from its carriage and sent it flying up in the air. The Rebel Cannoneers were ripped to pieces by the shrapnel from the exploding shell. The Cannoneer holding the lanyard was blown backwards jerking it as he flew through the air. This resulted in the Rebel Cannon discharging its round in its upward flight. The projectile sailed high, very high, right towards the mountaintop just behind and to the right of the Union lines.

Mark and Gabe were awakened by the sound of the Rebel cannon fire going up the valley. They scurried out from their little cave and scrambled atop the rocks. The boys watched as the Union cannon returned fire and saw the resulting explosion up the valley as the Union shell burst there.

There was an eerie sound, sort of like what a freight train makes as it rumbles down the tracks. It was combined with a whistling noise that seemed to grow louder and louder. A bright flash of brilliant orange and white light enveloped the area where the boys were. Then there was total darkness and silence.

Chapter XIX
The Awakening

The sun had come up fully when James woke up. The little cave was filled with the light of the morning sun. He looked around him and saw his brothers and Danny all sleeping.

"Wake up!" He cried. "Mark, you and Gabe were supposed to be on watch! C'mon, we gotta get up there and see what's goin' on. They're dependin' on us down there."

He scrambled over the stirring bodies of the others and scrambled up on the rocks. He put his telescope to his eye and looked up the valley. There were no Rebel troops to be seen. He swung around to look at their own fortifications and was surprised to see the place abandoned.

He dropped the telescope from his eyes and looked around in amazement. "What is goin' on?" he thought. I can barely see over the trees to the river! Danny, Mark, Gabe, get up here quick!"

The boys emerged from the little cave rubbing the sleep from their eyes. "I'm sorry James." Gabe said. "I must have fell asleep."

"Hush" said James. "Something's really strange here. Come up here and have a look see."

The boys climbed up on top and looked through their telescopes. "Where's everybody at?" Mark asked.

"They all must have skedaddled last night. I didn't hear any fightin!" Danny said.

"The Rebs are gone too" said James. "Something must have happened. I remember the cannon fire but I must have fallen asleep right after that. Did any of you hear anything?"

"No, nothin' at all, I slept like a baby."

James pondered for a moment. "Sgt. Myers said that if a retreat was necessary they were gonna head for Ravenswood. Let's eat a little breakfast and head that way."

"I wonder why those two Privates didn't come and get us," asked Gabe.

"Maybe they did come up and we didn't hear 'em or else the Rebs got 'em or maybe they didn't have time to come up. Who knows? We'll find out when we get to Ravenswood."

Chapter XX
Missing in Action / October, 1862

It was very hot that morning as Doctor Philson mounted his horse and headed from Racine up to Letart Falls. He was dreading this trip, but felt it was his duty to visit the McPhersons and the Wheelers. He got leave from the regiment to return home. In his saddlebag was a stack of unopened letters addressed to the boys. He was returning them.

As he neared the McPherson house, he saw Lorena standing on the porch watching him approach. "Well hello Doctor Philson, What brings you up this way?"

"I'm afraid I have some bad news for you Lorena," he said as he dismounted his horse and tied it to the hitching post, "Is your Ma & Pa home?"

With her heart in her throat, she sobbed, "Yes, please come in." He entered the house and was met by Mr. McPherson.

Noticing the look on his daughter's face and the solemn look of Dr. Philson, he said. "Doc, is somethin' wrong?"

"Is somethin' wrong with Danny?" sobbed Catherine, also sensing something wrong with Doctor Philson's demeanor.

"Ed, Catherine, Lorena, Danny's missing."

Lorena gasped, "Is Gabe all right?"

"There all missing." replied Dr. Philson.

"What can you tell me Doc?" asked Ed as he put his hand on the Doctor's shoulder.

"Well, there was a big fight over near Charleston. From what information I could gather by talking to the First Sergeant, they were sent out as Videttes to watch for the enemy's movement. The Rebs held off until almost dawn to begin their attack. The First Sergeant said they never did get a signal from the boys so he figured they had deserted. He said he had sent two men to fetch them back but they never returned either. The Rebs breached the works and we were forced to retreat amid great confusion."

"Now there are no confirmed reports the boys are anything other than missing. They may have gotten lost or even captured. We still have over thirty men listed as missing. I pray that they'll turn up soon. I just wanted you to know."

"I brought these letters back to you to hold for them. There's no need to send anymore until we can find them. I am so sorry."

Lorena screamed, "NO! NO!" She bolted out the door and ran as fast as she could with tears streaming down her face. She headed for Arcadia. When she arrived, she threw herself face down on the rock, cried, and prayed. She prayed for the safety of her beloved Gabriel, her brother Daniel and Mark and James.

"Oh God, please deliver them from whatever evil has befallen them. Please bring them home to us! Please bring my Gabe home to me!"

Doctor Philson departed the McPherson with promises to write to them if he heard anything further. He gently kicked his horse in ribs and headed him towards the Wheeler house.

Erissa and the children were staying at the Wheeler house while Mark was away. Little John and Little Isaac were climbing the apple trees in the orchard when they saw Lorena running through the meadow crying. They knew something was terribly wrong, as they had never seen her act like that before. They climbed down from the tree they were in and ran back to the house to tell their grandpa what they had just seen.

Elva said she would watch the boys. Erissa and John started out the door to go to Arcadia to see what was wrong with Lorena. That's when they saw Doctor Philson riding up the path towards the house.

"Oh no!" exclaimed Erissa, "Somethin's wrong with Ma or Pa."

"Doc, is there somethin' wrong over at the McPhersons?

"Doctor Philson dismounted and said, "No John, I need to talk to you all."

Elva came out onto the porch. "Elva, why don't you have the boys go fetch some water for my horse."

"Go on boys, take the Doctor's horse and give him some water, then take him over to the barn and brush him down."

"Please folks, sit down, I have something to tell you."

Erissa sat down on the porch step and said, "What is it Doctor Philson? You look like you just lost your best friend."

In his hand was another bundle of letters. "The boys are missing John, all of them including Mark, Erissa."

John, who had been leaning against the porch railing, slid down and sat on the floor as Elva sat down in a chair and covered her face with her handkerchief. Erissa began crying.

"What does that mean Doc?"

"It means they can't be accounted for right now." He went on to tell them about the fight at Charleston, the information he received from the First Sergeant, the confusion during the retreat and the hope that they were either lost or captured.

"What do you think Doctor? John asked, "Do you think they're all right?"

"It's my opinion John, that if they don't show up soon there's a good possibility that they were captured and that's not such a bad thing. Those boys are resourceful and I'm sure they could handle themselves as prisoners. If they were taken captive, there's the possibility of exchange. I promise you that I will write

~ 137 ~

and let you know if any information turns up. I'm heading back to the Regiment tomorrow. They gave me a pass so I could come see you and bring you these letters."

"Lorena took it very hard. I think you should all go down there to Arcadia and try to comfort her. I really must be going now, got a lot of ground to cover and a short time to do it."

The boys brought the Doctor's horse over and as the Doctor mounted he said, "Be seein' you all, my prayers are with you and the boys. I'll write you as soon as I hear anything."

As the Doctor left, they all walked quietly to Arcadia. The McPherson's were already there. They were sitting on the rock with Lorena. Ed was holding her in her arms as she sobbed on his shoulder. John joined them and put his arm around Lorena's waist. They all sat there crying softly for quite a while.

Lorena sobbed, "He promised me he would return to me and we would be together forever. He said it was our destiny to be together that we were born for each other and God meant it to be that way."

"Lorena, I know my son. He has the same blood as his Grandfather. If he told you that, then nothin' on this earth would keep him from fulfillin' his promise. You, and us, have to maintain the faith that our boys will be comin' home."

Erissa made her way to her sister and put her hand on her shoulder. "Lorena, once Gabriel told me and Mark that he loved you more than anythin' in this world. He said he couldn't stand the thought that something might happen to you while he was away and that you wouldn't be here when he returned. You and I both have to be strong for our men. We have to be here for them when they come home."

Chapter XXI
The Years Creep Slowly By

"The years did creep slowly by for Lorena and the McPhersons and the Wheelers," said the old man, "They never received any letters from the boys or Doctor Philson."

"My, that storm seems to be getting worse rather than better. It's really pouring out there!"

Another crack of thunder rattled the windows again.

"Lorena never married." The old man continued, "She had quite a few men come to court her, but she would have nothing to do with any of them.

My Great Grandmother Erissa never married again either. She told me that her sister Lorena was probably the prettiest girl that ever lived in those parts. Many men got their hearts broken."

She said that Lorena always wore the pendant that Gabriel gave her and she spent most of her time at Arcadia, keeping it clean and beautiful. Her father and John Wheeler had offered to go ahead and build the house there, but she wouldn't have it. She told them to wait until the boys came home. She wanted her Gabriel to be there when it was built.

After John died, the Wheeler farm became the property of my Grandfather, Little John. He also bought the McPherson Place after Ed and Catherine passed away so nobody else would move into their house. All of them are buried there in that meadow in the little cemetery where Papaw Isaac is resting. I've been there a couple of times.

Erissa and Lorena lived with my Grandfather at the Wheeler house and helped raise quite a few children. Lorena would take each child down to Arcadia and tell them about Gabriel. She would even take them down there swimming, even up into her old age; she would dive right in there with them.

One of the children said, "Grandpa, is this the end of the story? Tell us some more."

Another loud clap of thunder echoed outside and the hail began anew as the old man said, "No this is not the end of the story child, in essence it's only the beginning."

Chapter XXII
Reuben Clark / Mystery on the Mountain / July 1925

Up the Elk River near the town of Clendenin lived a man named Reuben Clark. He had a wife named Clara and two of the most beautiful Red Bone Coonhounds you ever saw. One he named Trumpet and the other Bugler. Reuben loved those dogs, almost as much as he loved his wife. He also loved corn liquor and would do just about anything he could to get some. Of course, this made for a poor relationship with Clara and she was constantly harping on him about it.

They lived in an old cabin back up one of the hollars off of the Elk River. Reuben would work some at the coalmines, do a little trapping and fishing along the elk. He would sell the furs he got to George Mason who owned a little country store near Clendenin.

George supplemented his income from the store with a small still back up in the hills. He would sell a little "Shine" to some selected customers. Reuben Clark was one of his best customers. George and his wife Glenda really liked Reuben and they used to make some deals with him. They even let him run a tab on this moonshine purchases.

Now Reuben's favorite thing to do was to head off into the hills with his hounds and a big jug of "Shine". Especially on a Friday night after payday when he'd collect his pay from the mine, run home give most of it to his wife then go see George to pick up his jug. He and the dogs would then head for the hills.

The baying of the hounds as they chased a raccoon through the woods was like music to his ears. He loved to just sit back against a tree trunk, sip his "Shine" and listen to his dogs. He could tell by the way they "bugled" whether they had a coon on the run or had one treed.

He carried an old kerosene lantern with him on these hunts and along about midnight he'd call in his dogs and head back to the house for a lecture from Clara about the evils of drinkin' and runnin' around in the woods.

One particular Friday, Reuben went home with his pay and Clara met him at the door. "I suppose yer gonna head up into the hills tonight with your dogs and your jug!"

Reuben looked at her and said, "Well that's a fine idea Clara, I think I will."

She glared at him and said, "You're a no-count, worthless old drunk Reuben Clark and I ain't a gonna put up with you no more. You won't listen to me. You don't give a damn about me!"

"Yeah I do, Clara, I do, I love you, you're my wife!"

"Reuben, I've given you warnings so many times and still you won't listen to me!' I've had it with you. You don't do a damn thing around here! You leave it to me to tend the garden, cook and clean and everything else while you go up in the hills a drinkin! You ain't never gonna get me outta this here old hollar! I ain't gonna stay here with you and die here! I'm goin' over to my sister's and as far as I'm concerned, you can go up in them hills and live with your dogs!"

She reached in the doorway and picked up a suitcase she had packed. She shoved him roughly aside and strode off the porch and down the hollar.

"Aw Clara, com'on back here, I'll come home early tonight and take ya into town tomorrow and buy you a new hat or sumpthin'. What do ya say Clara, C'mon back, I love you."

She stopped long enough to turn around and shout, "Go to hell!"

Reuben went to the shed untied his two dogs and headed to George's store. When he got there, George said. "Hey Reuben, How the hell are ya?"

"Ain't doin' so good, Clara's done left me again! Said she's gonna go live with her sister this time. I swear if I wasn't a drinkin' man that woman would drive me to drinkin'."

"What're you gonna do Reuben, go after her?"

"Hell no I ain't a goin' after her. She told me to go to hell! I'm gonna let her sister put up with her for awhile and pretty soon she'll drive her out and she'll come a crawlin' back. I'm a goin' up in the hills. Where's my jug?"

"Here ya go Reuben", said George as he handed him a jug of shine. "Now don't drink too much of that tonight. With the state of mind you're in you might just fall off a cliff or somethin' and break your fool neck. I worry about you sometimes Reuben."

"Well George, thank ye for a worryin' about me, but sometimes I think I might be better off ifen that did happen."

"Things will work out ok Reuben, you just be careful and have yourself a good time."

Reuben started upstream but stopped. He looked down at his hounds and said, "You boys know every coon up in that holler and all along this river. I'm gonna take you someplace we've never been afore. The old lady ain't at home so I don't have to worry about getting' back anytime soon. Let's go this way for a change."

He headed downriver towards Charleston.

"Look at that bunch of hills boys, they start out short over there and look how high that one is over there. We can go up on the short one, follow the ridgeline, and end up on that big ole mountain over there. I'd kinda like to go up there and see what I can see. Com'on boys lets go."

The dogs strained against the ropes he had tied around their necks. They basically pulled him up the slope towards the ridgeline. They were sniffing the ground making woofing sounds as they tasted the scents they picked up.

"Whoa boys!" he yelled as they came to the top of a hill. "I need me a drink!" He uncorked his jug and took a long swallow.

"Whew! He exclaimed, "Now that's a good batch! Let's go!"

He continued the climb, stopping periodically to rest and take a snort of his "shine". It was almost dark when he stopped this last time.

"I'm gonna turn you loose here in a minute boys. I just want to sit here a spell." He uncorked his jug again and looked down over the valley below. He could see where the Elk and the Kanawha Rivers met. Right smack downtown in the middle of Charleston. "Whoo Wee! He exclaimed. What a view up here. I bet I could see the whole town if I could get up on top of that big ole mountain."

He reached over and untied the ropes off his dogs. They sat there on their haunches looking at him waiting for a command from him. "Alright, go on boys." The dogs went off running into the woods and up the ridgeline.

Reuben took a few more sips of his "shine" then fell asleep leaning up against an old fallen tree trunk.

The baying of the hounds woke him up and it was pitch black. It was a lot darker that he thought it was going to be. A cloud cover had moved in and blanketed the moon.

He could hear his hounds baying way off in the distance, up towards the top of that big ole mountain.

"They got some ole coon on the run!" He thought, "Bet that ole coon's never come up against anythin' like my boys afore, especially livin' way up there on this mountain. I doubt if anybody's ever brought their dogs up this high."

The hound's baying turned to bugling and Reuben said aloud, "Hot damn! They got him treed now!"

He struggled to light his lantern. When he finally got it lit, he grabbed his jug and held the lantern up over his head. It cast an eerie glow on the trees and bushes surrounding him. He picked a way to go and started walking.

His eyes soon became accustomed the light of his lantern. He kept walking upwards towards the sound of the hounds. With tree branches slapping him in the face and the sweat pouring down his back, he kept climbing. He would stop every now and then and take a swig from the jug.

As he neared the top of the big mountain, the hounds went silent. He stopped and pricked his ears expecting to hear them start up again. He heard nothing but the breeze blowing through the trees above his head.

"That ole coon must have got away from 'em" he thought, "I'll just sit here a while and maybe they'll pick up the trail again."

He sat down and rested his back against a tree. He uncorked the jug then thought better of it. He shook the jug and realized he had drunk almost half of its contents. He returned the cork and sat the jug on the ground beside him. He blew out his lantern to save kerosene and sat there in the darkness listening for his dogs.

He happened to glance upward towards the top of the mountain. To his surprise, he saw a light. It was a flickering light.

"*Someone's got a fire goin' up there,*" he thought. *I might just mosey up there and see what's what. Maybe they seen my dogs or maybe they got my dogs!*"

He started to light his lantern, then thought, "No, I'll sneak up there and take a look. Don't want them to know I'm comin' up ifen they're tryin' to steal my dogs."

He started to climb up the hill, being as quiet as he could be which was hard to do with all the "shine" he had consumed. He stumbled over roots a couple of times nearly falling down.

As he got up to where he could see the fire, he counted four men sitting around the fire talking. He couldn't make out what they were saying as he was too far away. It looked like they were all drinking something out of tin cups.

He couldn't see his dogs anywhere so he decided to go on up.

He called out, "Halloo there! You fellas mind if I come up and join you for a spell?"

Startled the men stood up and stared into the darkness.

"What's your name? What regiment are you with? Did Sgt. Myers send you up here? Are you Secesh?

"I ain't no succotash, and I ain't with no regimen, just me, Reuben Clark a lookin' for my dogs. I don't know no Sergeant Myers. I stay away from the police as much as I can."

One of the men yelled, "Come on in stranger, just be slow about it."

As Reuben neared the fire, he noticed the boys were all wearing blue uniforms. "Oh shit!" he thought. "Are you boys with the police?"

The boys just looked each other. "No sir, we're with the 4th. What are you doin' up on this mountain?" asked James.

"I brought my hounds up to chase some coons. That's all. If I'm buttin' in on somethin' I can just turn around and leave ifen you want me too."

Not quite convinced they weren't police he asked, "You lookin' for stills up here?"

"No said James, "We're lookin' for a way out of here. Do you live around here?"

"Yeah I do, I got me a cabin up the Elk there, up in a hollar."

"How'd you get up here?" Mark asked.

"Just followed the ridgeline and ended up here."

The boys looked at each other again. "We tried that before." Mark said, "And we ended up right back here. We've walked every which way you can imagine and we always end up back here."

Reuben said, "Sounds to me like you're lost. All you gotta do is walk towards them city lights down there."

Reuben turned and pointed a shaking hand down the mountain towards Charleston. To his surprise, there were no lights. Just total darkness down in the valley.

James asked, "Want some coffee stranger?"

"Call me Reuben, I don't like bein' a stranger. Yeah, I'll have a cup." He glanced nervously back towards where the lights of Charleston should have been. "Hell, I think maybe I'm lost now."

"You can use my cup." James said as he poured Reuben a cup of smoking black coffee. He handed it to Reuben and as Reuben put it to his lips, he noticed the rifles the men had leaning up against the rocks behind them.

"Where in tarnation did you get them old rifles? I bet them's worth a lot of money! Look to be in purty good shape."

"Those were issued to us by the Army," said Danny.

"Army? There ain't no Army around here. What Army are you talkin' about?"

"Why the Union Army!" said Danny. "Do you think we're with the Confederate Army?"

~ 147 ~

Reuben spit out his coffee when he suddenly realized what these fellows were trying to say. He felt fear rise in his chest.

"You fellers are just a playin' with me ain't ya? You shouldn't mess with an old man like that."

"No sir we're not playin' with you," said Mark, "We need your help. We need you to show us how to get down from this mountain and get to Ravenswood where we can join up with our regiment before they declare us deserters or somethin'!"

Reuben's eyes widened with fright. He sat the coffee cup down and said with a shaky voice, "I uh,,, I gotta go fellas,,, I left my lantern back there in the woods and I uh... hear my dogs a bayin' for me. I gotta go... I gotta go. I gotta get my dogs and get home afore the old lady gets there." He stood up and turned to walk away.

"Come back Reuben, stay with us tonight and show us how to get down in the mornin'"

"Can't fellers, I gotta go!"

He got up and walked slowly back down the mountain with a stiff back, anticipating them to jump on him, or shoot him in the back. All of a sudden, a lightning bolt flashed across the sky followed by a large crack of thunder that echoed through the hills.

Startled, Reuben stopped and looked back. The soldiers were standing, beckoning and calling him to return and help them find their way out.

He turned once more and began walking slowly towards the woods where he came into the clearing. He could see the light from the campfire dancing on the leaves of the trees above his head. Then in an instant, the light went out and he was in total darkness.

He again stopped and turned back towards the men. There was no sign of them. No campfire either. Nothing but that pile of big rocks. The hair stood up on the back of his neck. He turned towards the valley and saw it was filled with the lights of Charleston.

He let out a yell and took off running through the woods. He was so terrified that he ran right past his lantern and jug lying on the ground. It seemed as if he was in a nightmare with darkness closing all around him. Suddenly there was a flash of light as he collided with a tree knocking him senseless to the ground.

Sometime during the night, a thunderstorm had passed over. Reuben wasn't aware of it. He was knocked out cold as ice.

He awoke the next morning with his coonhounds licking his face. He quickly sat up and his head felt like it was going to explode. He could barely see out of his left eye. He put his hand to his head and there was a bump bigger than a hen's egg above his eye.

"Where you been boys?" He felt around in his knapsack and found the ropes. He quickly tied them around the dogs necks and said, "C'mon boys, let's get the hell outta here."

"Home boys! Home! He had to hold the dogs back some as they descended the ridgeline. He kept looking back over his shoulder to see if he was being followed. He was shaking like a leaf, terror still tugged at his mind. When he finally came out of the mountains, he hurriedly made his way to George's store.

George was sitting on the front porch of the store as Reuben came into view. "Glenda! Glenda! Get out here quick! Somethin's happened to Reuben!"

Glenda stepped out onto the porch and saw Reuben's blood covered face. She put her hand to her throat and said. "Get him up here on the porch, I'll fetch some water and clean up his head."

George tied up the dogs and helped Reuben up onto the porch. He sat him down in a chair.

"What happened boy, did you fall off a cliff like I said?"

"Please, please get me a drink George. I need one awful bad." He pointed a shaking finger at George and said, "George, you ain't gonna believe what happened up there last night."

"Alright, you just sit there in that chair and rest a minute. Whew, boy you sure do stink. Looks like you pissed yourself too. Glenda forget that water, I'm gonna take him out back and hose him off! See if you can find something for that cut on his head."

"Come on, get up, I'll help you round back."

He walked Reuben around back of the store and hooked up a garden hose. Glenda came out with some soap and some towels.

"Alright, get them stinkin' clothes off Reuben and I'll hose you down. Glenda, go back in and get me a pair of my old pants and an old shirt for Reuben and throw 'em on the porch. We're gonna burn his clothes. It looks like he's crapped his pants too."

Reuben stripped naked and George ran the garden hose all over him.

"Now take the soap and scrub yourself down real good."

When Reuben was finished scrubbing himself, George hosed him down again and handed him a couple towels. "Dry yourself off and I'll go get those clothes"

He came back and sat the clothes down on the ground. "When you're done here, come on inside."

Reuben finished drying off and put on the clothes. He stumbled up the porch steps and into the house.

"Come on in and sit down at the table. Glenda's gonna fry you some eggs."

George sat a glass down in front of Reuben and poured him a healthy shot of good whisky. Reuben emptied the glass in one gulp and held out the glass for another. George filled it and said, "Alright now, tell me what happened. Did you drink that whole jug?

"No sir, I didn't, Said Reuben defensively, "I only drank less that half of it."

Reuben began to tell George about how he saw the campfire up on top of the mountain; how he'd thought they might have stolen his dogs. He told him how he thought the four men were policemen because they were all wearing blue uniforms.

"They tole me they was in the Army George. I asked 'em what Army cause there ain't no Army around here. They said the Union Army. Said they was lost and wanted me to stay with 'em and take 'em to Ravenswood to join up with their rejiman."

"There must have been more of 'em around those hills cause they tole me they was the 4th. I didn't see any more."

"Then strange things started happenin'. The lights in Charleston all went out! Then the campfire went out and those men disappeared into thin air! The wind was a blowin' and there was thunder and lightnin' everywhere!"

"Then them lights in Charleston came back on. I was so scared I started runnin' down that mountain right into a tree or somethin'. My dogs woke me up this mornin'."

"What did those men look like?" asked George.

"They was just young boys, in their 20's I reckon, none of 'em had a beard or anythin'.

"They had these old rifles, looked like muskets. And they had shiny buttons on their coats and a big shiny belt buckles."

"Wait a minute Reuben." George got up from the table and went into the bedroom. He returned a moment later with a picture in an old frame. "Did they look like this Reuben?"

He held the picture up in front of Reuben's face. "That feller wasn't there, but they was dressed like him."

George said, "This was my grandfather; he served in the 4th Regiment of West Virginia Infantry in the Civil

War. This is very interesting Reuben, What else can you tell me about last night?"

"There was this little cave like in that big ole pile of rocks. Looks like them men had been sleepin' in there. One of 'em went in and brought out a bag that had some sugar to put in my coffee."

"Do you think they were ghosts or something Reuben?"

"I don't know if they was ghosts or not. I touched the hand of the one that handed me my coffee and his hand was warm. So was the coffee. No, I don't think they was ghosts I think they was just lost men, very strange men."

"Do you remember how to get up there? Can you take me up there?"

"No, no sir, I ain't ever goin back up there! You couldn't pay me enough to get me back up there. That place is not for me. It's too scary."

"So you do think they were ghosts!"

"I didn't say that! I don't know what they were. Alls I know is that I got the hell scared out of me and I ain't a goin' back! Ifen you want to go up there, you can go by yourself. Just follow the ridgeline off the small hill and you'll go right to it. I ain't never a goin' back up there!"

"Alright Reuben, eat your eggs and I'll pour you another drink."

Chapter XXIII
Discovery on the Mountain

George had a brother named Irvin who lived in Charleston and made his living building and selling houses. Whenever George went into Charleston on business, he would stop in and visit his brother.

Irvin and his wife Charlotte were very much the socialites in Charleston. Irvin was a Mason and he and Charlotte were members of different organizations including the Kanawha Valley Historical Society.

A week after Reuben's experience, George went in to Charleston to order some goods for his store and stopped in at his brother's house to say hello. While there, he recounted the story that Reuben had told him. Irvin was fascinated and Charlotte was exuberant for she had recently joined a discussion group formed by some ladies interested in Spiritualism.

She said, "We must all go up there and hold a séance!"

Irvin said, "I don't think you'll ever get those fine ladies of Charleston to go traipsing through the woods, especially up some mountain to hold a séance. You complain when you have to climb a flight of stairs!"

"Perhaps you're right Irvin, but it will be an interesting story to tell at next week's meeting."

George said, "Irvin, how about you and me going up there? I know ole Reuben is a drunkard, but I've known him for years and that man ain't scared of nothun'. Hell, he roams through the woods at night. There's bear up in them hills. Never before did I hear him say he was scared up there. Now he won't go out at all. He even sold his beloved coon dogs!"

"I wish you could have seen him that morning he came down off that mountain. He was shaking like a leaf and it wasn't from the "shine" he'd been drinking.

I could see the fear in his eyes. There's something strange going on up there and I'd like to go up and see. What do you say? Do you want to go with me?"

Irvin sat there thinking for a moment.

"Yeah George, I will go up there with you and if you don't mind I'm gonna ask a friend of mine to come along. His name is Dave Spencer. He knows everything there is to know about the Civil War, especially the happenings around these parts. He's one of the officers at the Historical Society. He and I were going to go play some golf this Saturday, but once I tell him this, I'm sure he'll want to forgo the golf game and come up there with us. We'll be out to your house about 7am Saturday. Be ready to go."

"I will be Irvin. Tell this Spencer fellow to wear old clothes and a good pair of boots."

George was up and ready to go when he heard his brother's model T pull up in front of the store. "Glenda, I'll be back later on this afternoon."

"Be careful George. Don't you go falling of a cliff or anything. Bye Bye." He went outside and walked over to his brother's car as the men inside were getting out.

George, this here is David Spencer, Dave, my brother George. "I'm pleased to meet you."

"Same here." That's quite a tale your brother told me George. What do you think we'll find up there? Do you think the old man was just seeing things brought on by strong drink?"

"I don't rightly know what we'll find, but something mighty strange is going on up there. I've known ole Reuben for a long time and whatever he experienced up there changed his life. He doesn't hunt any more. Sold his dogs of all things! They were his prized possessions."

"He doesn't come around here much anymore. He just sits up there in his cabin in the hollar. Comes out and works at the mine once in a while to earn enough money to buy himself some supplies. What's that you got there Mr. Spencer?"

"You don't have to call me Mister George, call me Dave. This here is called an entrenchment tool. The Army issued them to our boys during the War. It's just a small shovel that folds up and I thought it might come in handy in case we want to dig around for artifacts or something."

"That's a good Idea, Dave, I packed up some stuff for us to eat for lunch and a couple jugs of water."

Irvin smiled at his brother and asked, "You sure its water in those jugs George? Come on, let's get started. I'll carry one of them jugs George."

"Dave said, "And I'll get the other one." Lead us on George. Do you know how to get there?"

"I believe so Dave, Reuben said to climb the short hill then follow the ridgeline up and we'll come right to it."

"Oh my God!" exclaimed Irvin as they approached the small hill. "Look at that! Those hills don't seem that high when you look up from down there in Charleston but from here they look like they're insurmountable!"

George replied, "If Old Reuben could make it up those hills, we should be able to."

After about three hours of climbing and walking upwards along the forested ridgeline, the men decided to take a rest. They popped the corks on the jugs and each took a swig.

"Yuck! It is water!"

"That's what I told you Irvin, I don't make the "shine" any more."

They sat in the cool shade for while talking. Looking down over the valley below, they could see part of the city of Charleston.

"This was different back in 1862 said David, "Charleston was just a small town, barely 1500 people.

There were more soldiers in the area than there were civilians."

"There was quite a fight around these parts. It ended up with the Yanks having to retreat up to Ravenswood. I have some firsthand accounts of this fight at home. I talked to a couple of old soldiers myself."

"I was looking through my files last night. A few years ago, I talked to an old gentleman from up around Greenbriar. His name was Crawford, Rafe Crawford. He told me the Signal Corps had been moved east with Cox. They had left one of their wagons behind loaded with some of their gear."

"Lightburn wanted videttes on top of some of the high points to watch for movement of the Rebels. Rafe said they had no experienced signalmen so the First Sergeant chose men from the ranks to send up in the hills. Rafe and several others were assigned to watch for signals from them."

"Rafe said the Rebs opened up an hour-long artillery bombardment the day they sent the men up into the hills and that evening a shorter one. Expecting a full-scale assault in the morning, Lightburn ordered a retreat later that evening which resulted in utter chaos."

"Men were sent to retrieve the videttes. Rafe said he and another private were headed up into the hills. When they arrived, they found all four of these videttes dead. Knowing the retreat was on, he said they placed the bodies in a small cave along with what equipment they could find. They covered up the mouth of the cave with stones and brush to keep the animals from getting to the bodies. He said it was their intent to report the location so the bodies could be retrieved later."

"As they were going back down the mountain, they were surrounded by Rebel skirmishers and captured. They ended up being sent to Andersonville where the other private died of sickness. Rafe said he nearly died too. He said he never gave much thought after the war about those men they put in the cave. He said he'd seen so much death and sickness that he completely put it all out of his mind until our conversation brought some of those memories back."

"I had forgotten about this too until Irvin told me about Reuben's story. It really got me to thinking. I'm not one to believe in ghosts or anything like that, but I've heard some pretty strange tales in my life... things that couldn't be explained. I got this eerie feeling that we're going to find something up there."

George said, "Let's go then."

After walking upwards for about a half an hour George exclaimed, "Look here boys, here's old Reuben's lantern and his jug!"

The globe had been broken in the lantern. The cork was still in the jug. George popped it and held it to his nose. "Whew, this stuff's rancid! He poured the contents out. "Old Reuben wasn't lying? He had drunk only about half this jug. Look there, just beyond those trees up ahead! I can make out those rocks he was talking about! Com'on let's go!"

He hurriedly put the jug in his sack and took off towards the rocks. Irvin and Dave were right behind him. As they scrambled upwards, the woods began to thin out a bit. They finally stepped out into a clearing and there in front of them was the huge pile of big rocks that Reuben had said he'd found.

George went to the rocks and climbed up to the top. "Come on up here and let's eat lunch before we go diggin' around." As the other two climbed up he said, "Just look at that view. Why you can almost see all the way up both valleys! I didn't think Charleston was so big! Look! There's the Elk and there's where she flows into the Kanawha."

"Beautiful!" Dave exclaimed, "Just beautiful!"

George reached into his sack and pulled out some ham sandwiches that Glenda had made. He handed them out and was saying, "Got some boiled eggs here too and got an onion somewhere down in there. Here it is, want a slice of onion to put on your sandwich?"

"I do, slice me off a thin piece," said Irvin.

David said, "I'll pass, want some water?"

After they ate their lunch and washed it down with water from Dave's canteen, George started to stand up and in doing so, kicked his pocketknife he had laid down beside him after he peeled and sliced the onion. It went skittering down the rock and rolled into a crevice.

"Oh hell, I gotta get that back, Glenda got me that knife for my birthday."

He got down on his hands and knees and scooted himself down the boulder. He reached into the crevice and his hand touched something other that his knife. He took hold and pulled out an old brass telescope.

"Look here what I found" he exclaimed. "This thing's older than hell, still works though, well it would work if the front lens wasn't busted."

"Let me see that, said Dave. He turned it over in his hands and said, "Here's an inscription. It says, Signal Corps, 4th Regiment." The telescope, which was weathered badly, was fully extended and would not compact.

"This is quite a find George! Let's see what else we can find up here." The men started reaching in the numerous cracks and crevices in that big pile of rocks.

"Look! Here's some kind of button, got an eagle on it!" Here's another one!"

"Here's what's left of a tin cup", said Irvin.

I got something here boys," said David. He was laying flat on his stomach reaching way down between two big boulders.

"Can't quite reach it." he groaned.   He shifted himself a little closer and reached in again. "Here we go, need to work it out real slow, some kind of cloth." He finally pulled out the tattered remains of a white flag. It was very flimsy and tore easily. There was a red square sewn in the middle of it.

"A signal flag! Ain't that something! A signal flag that's been layin' up here for over 60 years! This is great! It feels like we're going back in time!"

He laid the flag down and picked up his e-tool. As he slid down the rock, he said, "I'm going down there and look around."

He began scraping away some dirt and debris from the base of the rocks, slowly working his way around it. Suddenly he looked up and the strangest feeling came over him. There in front of him was a pile of small rocks stacked up against the main pile.

"George, Irvin, come down here and see this! I think I found something!"

The two scrambled down off the rocks. "What, what is it?"

"There! Look there! Remember what I told you old man Crawford said to me? About putting those dead soldiers in a cave and covering it up with stones? What's that look like to you?"

"Only one way to find out" said Irvin as he picked up one of the stones and tossed it down the hillside. "Come on!"

The men began clearing the stones away. Soon they could see the entranceway of a small cave or an opening formed by the two biggest boulders in the pile leaning against other.

"We're almost there."

David cleared the last few rocks away and crawled inside the little cavern. He quickly backed out and with a strange look on his face. He stood and said, "Boys, we need to put those rocks back. They're in there, or what's left of them are in there. Looks like four of 'em. We need to bring some more men up here and get them out. They replaced most of the stones, picked up their gear and headed back down the mountain.

"Looks like Crawford was telling the truth" said David.

"Looks like Reuben wasn't lying' either", said George.

None of them did much talking on the way back to George's store. Each was lost in his own thought.

Chapter XXIV
Recovery / Identification

With the storm still raging outside, the old man paused long enough to refill and light his pipe again. "It's gettin' chilly in here! Casey, you and John need to go get some more wood for the fire. If anyone has to go to the bathroom, go do it now. I'll wait until everyone's back before I continue."

There was a scramble as people hurried to the bathroom or to the kitchen for a snack. Amy got a glass of iced tea and brought it over to the old man. She handed it to him and sat down on the floor beside him.

"Thank you darling. I needed somethin' to wet my whistle."

"Dad, is this story really a true story? Why didn't you ever tell me before?"

"Well Honey, I never felt the time was really right to tell anyone until now. I sort of made a promise to someone long ago to leave it be. Now I'm gettin' old and I think it would be the wrong thing to do if I took this to my grave. I'm the only one left that knows this story."

Casey and John brought in an armful of kindling and began putting some of it into the fire. The rest they stacked on the floor beside the fireplace.

Kelli came in with a piece of apple pie for her Father. "Don't you have to go to the bathroom Dad?"

"I will after I eat this pie; thank you darlin'."

Linda said, "Oh I wish this storm would let up and the power would come back on. Do you think we need more candles?"

"I hope it storms all night," said Amy, "Don't you Dad?"

The old man swallowed the last bite of pie and said, "You bet ya! There ain't nothing like a good thunderstorm. Helps you sleep!"

Everyone was back and the old man said, "Now it's my turn to go to the bathroom. I'll be right back."

As he made his way through everyone sitting or laying on the floor Kelli turned to Linda and said. "Don't you just love it? He's doin' so well tonight. I haven't heard him talk so much in a long time.

"Must be something in that turkey you fixed Mom," said Amy.

"I think it was the cranberry sauce," said John, "he really wolfed that stuff down."

They chuckled and Kelli said, "That's my Dad, the one I used to know."

The old man came back and took his place by the fire. "Where was I?" he asked as he re-lit his pipe. "Oh yeah, now I remember."

July 15, 1925

There were quite a few cars and pickup trucks parked around George's store that morning. David and Irvin got some local high school boys to volunteer to go back up on the mountain with them to help bring the soldiers down. Reverend Jamison was going to accompany them. A few younger members of the Historical Society were planning to make the climb up the mountain. There were also quite a few spectators milling around and up on the hill behind the store sat old Reuben, sipping from a jug of "shine". He'd taken to drinking again. He had told George that morning, "Now ya believe me don't cha. I weren't lyin' to you just to get a drink. I'll pay you for this here jug when Clara gets back I promise."

"Don't worry about that Reuben, this jug is on the house. Don't tell anyone I still have some."

The Charleston Gazette was to have a reporter there that morning to accompany the group up the mountain. They were waiting for him to arrive. He finally pulled up and parked his car.

David climbed up on the porch and yelled, "Listen, everyone who's going up that mountain with us! I want to tell you right now that this is not like an evening stroll. Going up that mountain is hard work. If you don't have a canteen of water, I suggest you buy a jug from the store here and fill it up. There's a tap out back. It's going to be a long, hard, hot walk and we don't want to have to end up carrying any of you back down that mountain."

"Now you younger boys and men, if you get to the top before the rest of us you are not to touch a stone or a blade of grass before we are all there. I don't want any of you playing around up there. This is a solemn occasion and those men deserve our respect. We're leaving here in 15 minutes."

The group started up the hill and soon the older ones were lagging back. The boys were whooping and hollering as they started out on a run, but soon the uphill climb got to them also and the group was spread out for almost a quarter of a mile. They had to stop several times to rest and drink.

It was well past noon before the first of the young boys reached the top. True to their word, they sat down in the shade of some trees at the edge of the clearing and waited for the others.

A few of the men arrived and a couple of them went into the woods and cut eight long sturdy poles. They made four stretchers by placing a blanket between two poles, poking holes in the edge of the blanket and tying it securely with rawhide.

Finally, the last of the group struggled in and after a moment respite, the Reverend Jamison said a prayer.

"Father, we ask that you bless our work here. We know that you have taken the souls of these brave men home to be with you long ago. We ask that you help us to find their families, if any are left here on this earth, so that there may be peace in their hearts and that the bodies of these young men be laid to rest in with the remains of their families who loved them and worried about them for so long. Amen."

They walked to the rocks and began removing the stones from the cave entrance. Two young men were selected to go into the cave.

"Boys, bring out one body at a time and whatever is lying next to them."

The boys entered the cave and soon emerged with the skeletal remains of the first soldier. His blue uniform although tattered and falling apart was still mostly intact around the body. His belt was still in place and he was still wearing his shoes. They laid him gently on the first stretcher and re-entered the cave.

They came back out with the remains of a knapsack, a hat and a telescope. They laid these items on the stretcher with the remains of the soldier.

One of them said, "There's lots of stuff in there, all scattered about. Looks like someone just throwed it in there. There's a couple of rusted old rifles and some old canvas bags. Can't tell which one they belonged to by where they're layin."

"Alright," said David, "Let's just bring the bodies out now. Maybe we can figure that out later."

One by one, the boys brought out the remains and laid them on the stretchers. They cut some more poles and made another stretcher to carry the remaining artifacts they found in the cave. There were the two rifles, another telescope, three more knapsacks, two bayonets and several pieces of tin cookware.

The group stayed pretty much together on their downward trek off the mountain. It was a much quieter group. When they arrived at the store, the remains were placed in a pick up truck and driven to "Moore's Funeral Home" in Charleston.

The next morning the Charleston Gazette carried the following article:

REMAINS OF UNION SOLDIERS REMOVED FROM MOUNTAIN
Charleston, July 15th, 1925

The remains of four Union soldiers who were killed in 1862 during the Battle of Charleston were removed from Kanawha Mountain this day. According to David Spencer, noted Charleston historian, these men were probably soldiers of the 4th Regiment of West Virginia Infantry. They were found buried in a rock formation atop the mountain. They had been resting there for over 60 years when they were found by Mr. Spencer along with Irvin Mason of Charleston and his brother George from Clendenin who had climbed the mountain last week in search of Civil War artifacts. Some sources say it was actually Reuben Clark, a coal miner from Clendenin, who first found the site where the bodies were entombed. His story led the others to go there in search of artifacts. The remains are being stored in Moore's Funeral Home. Mr. Spencer and others from the Kanawha Historical Society will try to identify them and if successful will attempt to locate any living family members for disposition of the remains.

When they arrived at the funeral home, the remains and artifacts were taken into one of the back rooms. David and the Mason brothers along with several members of the Historical Society decided to meet there the next day and examine everything to see if they could somehow identify the bodies. The doors of the funeral house were locked and David asked the police department to post a guard so that no unscrupulous souvenir hunter could gain entrance during the night and disturb the bodies or steal any of the artifacts.

The next morning the examination began by going through the knapsacks. They took the knapsack of the first soldier brought out and opened it gently. There was nothing much inside, the remains of a few letters, but they were entirely unreadable. They had gotten wet over the years and had crumbled to pieces. A wooden cartridge box, a spoon, a quill pen and a small bottle of ink were found. There was nothing that offered any clue as to the soldier's name or unit. Examination of the remaining knapsacks brought the same results.

David stood and said, "Gentlemen, let's see what we can find on the remains."

They laid one of the stretchers upon the table. David gently turned the skeletal remains so the soldier was lying on his back.

"Here's something," said David, in the soldier's left breast pocket was a small leather pouch. David gently pulled it from the pocket and when he did, there was a cascade of small silver coins that fell upon the table. He picked one up and examined it closely.

"A silver 3 cent piece! There must be 20 or 30 of them here!" He turned the pouch over and said, "There's some kind of writing on this piece of leather. It is hard to make out. Looks like the letters were burnt in."

The age of the leather made the burned markings nearly invisible. He took it over to the sunlight coming in from the window and began to examine it again.

After a moment he looked up and exclaimed, "Gabriel, Gabriel Wheeler, It says "Gabriel Wheeler, Letart Falls O, from Lorena at Arcadia 1861. Gentlemen, I believe we have the name of our first soldier."

"We can't be sure about that David," said Irvin, What if he stole that pouch?"

"That may be true I...wait, why didn't I think of this before! Sometimes soldiers carved their name or initials on the back of their belt buckles!"

He hurried back over to the table. He placed his fingers underneath the belt buckle and turned it over. There, carved on the back of the buckle was the following: "Gabriel Wheeler, Letart Falls, O and Arcadia".

"There is the proof. That is all I need. Gentlemen, meet Mr. Gabriel Wheeler."

They examined and got the names of the other soldiers off their belt buckles.

George said, "Looks like 3 brothers and a friend or a cousin. All of them said Letart Falls, Ohio. Where is that?"

One of the Society members said, "Letart Falls is a little farming community downriver from Ravenswood on the Ohio side. I've been there a couple of times to buy tomatoes."

"Still think they were in the 4th West Virginia Infantry David? I mean being they were all from Ohio, you'd think they might be from an Ohio regiment. Were there any Ohio regiments in that fight?"

"Yes, there was, but the 4th had three or four full companies made up of men from Ohio. A lot of them from Meigs County and that's where Letart Falls is located if it's where you say it is. I'm going to check the 4th's muster records first."

The next morning around 10, David took a walk to the Capitol Building complex. The air was cool and the sky overcast. The morning dew was still heavy on the grass. He carried a briefcase, which contained pen and paper, notes on what he had found and the file he had on Rafe Crawford.

The State Archivist and Record keeper was Clifford Myers. David had known Clifford for years and had developed a close friendship as they both shared an intense interest in Civil War history.

As he neared the steps leading into the Archives Building, he paused to reflect for a moment on what happened. He lit a cigarette and as the white smoke swirled about his head, he thought, "I wonder if there are any family members left alive over there in Letart Falls who knew these boys? It would be great if there were someone who could tell me about these boys and their lives before the war. I can foresee a book on this maybe, plus it may give some closure to that person as to what happened to them."

He formed a mental picture of the four boys and imagined what they might have looked like all decked out in their uniforms of blue. He imagined the sound of their voices when they spoke, their patriotic intensity. He tried to imagine their individual personalities. He finished his cigarette and turned to walk up the stairs.

He opened the door, stepped inside the building and walked up to the receptionist's desk.

"Can I help you?" asked the pretty, dark haired young girl sitting behind the desk.

David took notice of her name on the nameplate setting on her desk. It read "Patricia Crenshaw."

"Yes Miss Crenshaw, I was wondering if Mr. Myers might be in."

"And your name sir"?

"I am David Spencer, a friend."

"Mr. Spencer, of course, he has been expecting you."

She noticed the puzzled look on David's face as she pushed the intercom button." "Mr. Spencer is here to see you sir".

"Great!" Came the reply," I'll be right out."

David heard a door open and close down the hallway and the footsteps of Clifford approaching.

"Hello Dave" said Clifford, "I thought maybe you might be here soon. I read the article in the paper about your find; very exciting!"

"Hello Cliff", David replied as he held out his hand.

Cliff took his hand and with a firm grip said, "I was going to pay you a visit this evening if you didn't show up here today. Come on back to my office. I have been pulling what records we have from the 4th West Virginia Infantry."

As they started down the hallway, Cliff turned to his receptionists and said, "Patty, hold all my calls for a while."

"Yes sir, Mr. Myers."

As Cliff opened his office door and entered, he motioned to a chair in front of his desk.

"Have a seat Dave, tell me what you know about these bodies you found."

"We have names Cliff, and we know these boys were from Ohio. I was wondering if you could help us find out more about them through the records you might have."

"Wonderful, wonderful, you have names; we have most of the muster records and enlistment sheets from the 4th. I have already pulled what I could find. It may take a while, as there were seven full companies of the 4th that were recruited from Ohio.

"We know where they were from." David continued. "They had carved their names and hometown on the back of their belt buckles. They were from over in Meigs County, near Letart Falls. One of the boys had scratched the name Arcadia on his belt buckle. That may have been the name of a long ago little village or something. We haven't been able to locate that name on any maps."

"What names do you have Dave?"

"Gabriel Wheeler, J. Wheeler, M. Wheeler and D. McPherson. Gabriel was the only one to carve his full name."

Cliff began to shuffle through the yellowed sheets of paper on his desk, looking for the entry of Letart Falls.

"Here, here they are!" He said excitedly. He flipped one of the pages around and said, "Look just below my finger."

David leaned over and there, written in faded brown ink were the following names among about 50 entries on the sheet:

James Wheeler, age 27, from Letart Falls, O, Farmer, Carpenter
Daniel McPherson, age 25, from Letart Falls, O, Farmer
Mark Wheeler, age 25, from Letart Falls, O, Farmer
Gabriel Wheeler, age 19, from Letart Falls, O, Farmer

The top of the sheet read: Company E, Mustered in at Mason City, West Virginia July 22, 1861. David scribbled the information down on his notepad and said, "Well Cliff, looks like I'm going to be making a trip across the river; would you like to come with me?"

"I would love to go Dave, when do you want to go?"

"As soon as possible, the bodies are being kept over at Moore's Funeral Home and Mr. Moore is already complaining of the crowds that have been trying to get in over there to view the bodies. He wants them out as quickly as possible. The police department has provided a guard to protect them, but I don't know how long they will provide that service."

I can't go tomorrow; I have a Historical Society meeting to go to. How about Saturday morning?"

"Saturday is fine with me" said Cliff, "I'll drive; I just got a new Ford truck and would like to give it an extended test run anyway. I'll pick you up, say around 8 a.m.?"

"8 a.m. is fine," replied Dave as he jotted something down on his notepad. He tore off the sheet and handed it to Cliff.

"If you would like to view the bodies and the artifacts we found, take this over to the funeral home and give this to Mr. Moore. He will let you in."

Chapter XXV
Trip to Letart Falls / John's Run / The Wheeler House

Another loud crack of thunder rattled the windows and the old man paused. He began to repack his pipe and said, "This storm's not showing any sign of letting up!" Haven't seen one like this for a long time, won't be long before the streets are so flooded you won't be able to drive."

Casey got up and looked out the window as a flash of lightning lit up the area around the house. "Looks like they are already flooded Dad. Looks like we're all gonna have to spend the night here."

Linda said, "Well, we got plenty of food and more than enough blankets and pillows for everyone. John, you and Casey go get some more wood for the fire."

The old man said. "I'll wait until you get back before I go on with the story."

John and Casey scrambled out to the garage and returned with their arms full of firewood. They laid the firewood down on the hearth and put a few pieces in. John stoked the fire with the poker and soon had a good blaze going. "Ok Dad, we're ready."

July 18, 1925

David was sitting on his front porch when he heard a car coming up the street. A shiny brand new Ford Model T Runabout truck pulled up in front of his house. Cliff opened the door of the truck and waved at David. "Ready to go?" He was wearing a long coat, hat and a pair of goggles around his head.

"Nice truck you have there Cliff. What did that set you back for?" He asked as he walked toward the truck.

"$300.00" replied Cliff, I know that sounds like a lot, but look at all the room back there. I can cart around almost anything I need."

Dave put his suitcase in the bed of the truck and noticed a 5 gallon gas can. "Extra gasoline?" He asked.

"Yeah, I thought I'd better bring a can full. Not sure where I can get gasoline over there and once the fuel tank gets low you can't drive up some hills without putting it in reverse and backing up. I don't like to do that. I'd rather keep the fuel tank full as possible."

"I have decided to go from here to Ravenswood and cross on the ferry there. I'll fill the tank up in Ravenswood before we cross over. Here, put this coat and hat on, it will keep the dust from settling on your clothes. There's a pair of goggles in the pocket."

Dave put the coat on and thought, "Boy! Is this going to be a hot trip!" As he climbed into the truck, Cliff put it in gear and started down the street towards the Ravenswood road.

"How long do you think it will take to get there?" David asked.

"We should be in Ravenswood by noon if we don't run into any rain. Driving on dusty roads is better than driving on muddy roads. This truck will go as fast as 45 miles per hour, but that's on good roads. I don't know what condition the road to Ravenswood is in so I'll hold the speed down."

It was about 11:30 when they reached the outskirts of Ravenswood. The ride had not been too bad. There were a lot of bumps and potholes in the road, but no major problems.

Cliff pulled over by a general store and parked the truck by the gasoline pump. A man came out and asked how much he wanted. "Fill it up," said Cliff. He and David went inside the store as the man began to pump the gasoline.

"The gasoline and lunch is on me," said David.

"I won't argue with that," said Cliff.

The storekeeper entered the store and asked, "Anything else for you fellers?"

"Dave replied, "Yes, we'll have a pound of that bologna, a loaf of bread and two bottles of root beer. And we would like to have a small jar of mustard also please."

"Would you like that bologna sliced?"

"Yes please"

"Thick or thin?"

"Thick if you don't mind."

The storekeeper sliced their bologna and wrapped it in wax paper. He put it, along with a small jar of mustard, into a large brown paper bag and handed it to David. "The root beer is over there in that cooler and the bread is on the shelf behind you. That'll be one dollar and twenty five cents please."

David paid the storekeeper as Cliff went over to the cooler and pulled out two bottles of root beer. He then grabbed a loaf of bread off the shelf as he followed David out the door.

"Let's go on down to the ferry and have our lunch there" said Cliff.

"Fine with me" said David.

David got into the truck as Cliff went to the front to turn the crank to start the engine. He was surprised it started on the first crank. He climbed into the truck and started towards the ferry landing.

They proceeded into the town of Ravenswood and found the street that led down to the landing. They stopped on the hill above the landing overlooking the Ohio River and parked under a shade tree to eat their lunch.

The ferryboat was at the Ohio side of the river so they had a little time to kill before it returned to the West Virginia side. As they were eating Dave asked, "How are we going to locate these families?"

Cliff replied, "I looked up the name of the postmaster in Letart Falls, her name is Grace Roberts. She lives beside the post office so it shouldn't be too hard to find her. We'll see if she knows of any Wheelers or McPhersons in the area."

"I hope we can locate these boys' families but in a way, I hope we don't open up any old wounds that have healed with time. I wonder how they will react."

"David, whatever happens we'll know we did the right thing. If we are unable to locate any relatives then we will find out if we can have them interred in a local cemetery there. Those boys deserve a better resting place than atop that old mountain. At least they'll be coming home. If we can't get the local authorities to authorize this, then we'll go to the state of Ohio."

The ferry pulled away from the Ohio side and began chugging across the river towards Ravenswood. When it landed, the ferry master dropped the ramp and two automobiles and two horses pulling a wagon drove off the ferry. Cliff started his car and rolled down the hill towards the ferryboat. The ferry master waved for him to drive on.

"That'll be 25 cents," he said as he approached the car. "We'll be pullin' out as soon as we get a few more passengers. Where ya'll goin' to?"

"We're headed for Letart Falls. Do you know the best way to get there?"

"Jest go up to the road when I let you off and turn left. Foller that road and it'll take ya through Apple Grove and the next town ya come to is Letart Falls."

"Thank you sir" said Cliff.

"Thank you mister fer usin' my boat."

After about 20 minutes, two men on horseback and another car had boarded the ferry. The ferry master raised the ramp and fired up the engine. The ferry began its journey across the river. As they neared the Ohio landing, Cliff got out of the car and went to the front to crank up the engine. When he got the car started, the ferry master was lowering the ramp. He waved at Cliff and Dave as they drove off the ferry and headed up towards the road.

They turned left on the road and as they came to the first curve, David said, "Look there, looks like a storm brewing."

Cliff had already noticed the dark clouds forming on the horizon as they crossed the river.

"I hope it holds off until we get to Letart, this road's in pretty bad shape as it is. Hold on, I'm going to kick up the speed a little."

"Alright" said Dave as he tensed for an expected bump coming up, "but watch out for those potholes."

The ride from the ferry landing to the little hamlet of Apple Grove was a rough one. Along with many potholes and rocks there were major ruts in the road that were made by vehicles that had passed when the road was muddy.

The storm seemed to be moving away from them and Cliff and David both let out a sigh of relief when the road began to smooth out just before they reached Apple Grove. David said, "There were some very pretty farms along that road."

Cliff answered, "I wouldn't know, I couldn't take my eyes of the road long enough to look at anything else for fear of crashing. I'm gonna' slow her down now. This road's in pretty good shape and it looks like the storm is gonna' pass."

"I'm sure glad of that," said Dave, "I wonder how far it is to Letart Falls from here?"

"Not too far according to the map. This little town of Apple Grove sure is a pretty place isn't it. Not too many houses. Got a fine view of the river here. It would be a good place to retire to, start a little truck farm and do a lot of fishin'. I may look into that one of these days."

A couple miles past Apple Grove, they came upon a bridge crossing a creek that flowed down through the hills and into the Ohio River.

"Look at that, let's stop here for a minute." said David.

Cliff pulled to a stop and set the brake. "I bet there's some good fishing here!" He said as he opened his door and stepped out.

There was an area of water that covered a couple of acres where the creek backed up. The two men gazed out over the water.

"Look there!" said Cliff, "See that bass goin' after that bluegill? He came clear out of the water. I sure wish I'd brought my fishin' pole with me. If we come back here again, I'll have it next time for sure."

A big Blue Heron glided in over the treetops and landed on the far bank.

"Looks like he's after some supper" said David. "We'd better get moving." They got back in the car and started down the road.

"Wonder what the name of that creek is? Cliff asked.

"The sign back there said, "John's Run," replied David.

"Well, looks like we have arrived." Cliff said as they passed a road sign that said Letart Falls.

There were quite a few houses along both sides of the road. They passed an automobile service station and Cliff said, "Looks like I didn't have to lug along that extra gasoline after all." Look, there's another one comin' up."

"And there's the Post Office on the other side" said David.

The road forked right there with the right hand fork making a hard right and other fork going slightly to the left. Cliff took the left hand route and stopped in front of a large building.

"Looks like the Post Office is part of this store and its open for business" said Cliff as he pulled to a stop and shut the engine off. Let's go inside"

They walked up the wooden steps to the porch in front of the store. David opened the screen door and held it open for Cliff. "After you sir."

"Thank you sir" replied Cliff. David let go of the door just as Cliff started to enter and the spring that held the door shut, caused the door to slam shut on Cliff's backside.

"Sorry said David, "Just paying you back for that rough ride over here."

Cliff smiled as he pushed the door open and held it for David to enter. The inside of the store was rather dark and cool. The air was filled with the smell of fresh bread and other bakery goods. There were shelves lined with canned goods and other items.

An older woman approached them and asked, "Can I help you gentlemen?"

"We're looking for the Post Office," said David.

"I'm sorry sir; the Post Office is closed until Monday."

"Actually" said Cliff, "We're looking for the Post Master.

"In that case I can help you. My name is Grace and I am the Post Master here in Letart Falls, what can I do for you?"

Cliff said, "I am Cliff Myers, Archivist for the State of West Virginia and this is David Spencer, noted author. We are also members of the Kanawha Valley Historical Society and you must be Grace Roberts.

"I am indeed," she said, "I'm please to meet you fine gentlemen."

"Mrs. Roberts..." Cliff began,

She held up her hand and interrupted. "Please call me Grace."

"Grace, we are in the possession of the remains of four soldiers from the Civil War and we believe they are from this area. We are anxious to find out if there are any relatives who would claim the bodies and give them a decent burial.

"The State of West Virginia would be happy to cover the costs of transporting the remains and the burial. We have the names of the individuals. Three of them carried the last name of Wheeler and the other one was a McPherson. Is there anyone around here who carry those names?"

"Oh my Lord!" exclaimed Grace as she put her hand to her throat. "Oh my Lord!" she repeated as she motioned the men to follow her. "Come, sit down for a spell."

She led them over by an old coal-burning stove that had several old wooden chairs around it. She sat down in one and motioned for the men to sit.

"There are two sisters who live up above John's Run. One is named Erissa Wheeler and the other is Lorena McPherson. There's a story told around here about what happened to those two families back during the Civil War. The Wheelers and McPhersons were neighbors back up the run.

Erissa was a McPherson who married one of the Wheeler boys. Her younger sister Lorena was going to marry one of the other ones when the war broke out. The Wheeler boys and the McPherson boy all left for the war and never returned.

"Lorena never married. I've been told, she was considered to be a fine looking woman in her youth. She broke a lot of hearts. They say she never took another interest in men after her fiancé failed to come home."

"The McPherson house burned down quite a few years ago and Lorena moved in with her sister at the old Wheeler home. That land is owned and farmed by

"Little John Wheeler" now, except for one area, which belongs to Lorena. She calls that area Arcadia."

"I've heard people talk about that place. Those that have seen it say it's like nothing else around these parts. They say that even on the hottest days it's as cool as a cucumber there. They say even the animals aren't afraid to come there to drink while Lorena is present. I've never seen it; she talks about it from time to time when she and her sister come to the store to buy things. She won't let just anybody go there."

"Was her fiancé named Gabriel?" David asked.

"I'm not quite sure," answered Grace, but I believe that was the name of one of the Wheeler boys."

"I found a leather pouch on one of the bodies that had burned onto it "To Gabriel from Lorena at Arcadia."

"How do we get to the Wheeler house?" asked Cliff.

"Go back the way you came, towards Apple Grove. You'll cross over the bridge there at John's Run and there is a small road on the left, just past that bridge. That road runs up past the Wheeler place. It's about a half a mile or so up that road I reckon."

The distant rumble of thunder made Cliff look up at the window. "Let's get going Dave, looks like that storm is turning around and headed back this way."

"We need a good rain." said Grace, "But I hope it holds off until you get there."

"This is going to be big news around here gentlemen, but I am not going to say anything to anyone about it until you return here and let me know how things work out. I wouldn't want people to go running up there and bothering those people about it if they are not welcome, so please promise me you'll return and let me know what's going on with this before you leave to go back to Charleston."

"We promise Grace, you've been a big help."

Cliff cranked the truck and got it started. He climbed in and headed back towards Apple Grove. They came to the bridge at John's Run and located the road just where Grace said it would be. As Cliff turned on to the road, he stopped the truck.

"Oh my!" he said, look at that! And you thought the road from the landing to Apple Grove was bad!"

David took one glance up the road and said, "Maybe we should park here and walk up to the house."

"Naw," said Cliff, "I'm game to give it a try." He put the truck in gear and bounced up the road at a crawl.

"May be a little rough, but it sure beats walking!"

The sky above them began to darken and the wind was making the maple trees turn their leaves belly up as if beckoning the rain from the heavens. As they topped a small hill, they could see the Wheeler house a short distance ahead.

"What a beautiful house!" exclaimed David! "Setting up here in the hills like that! Look at that farmland and that meadow out back. Sure is lovely."

"Look! Cliff said, "I bet that's Lorena and Erissa sitting there on the porch."

"Watch out! David yelled, as an old man with a white beard stepped out onto the road from behind a brush pile. Cliff swerved just in time. The old man just stood there and watched them.

"That was close" Cliff said, I didn't see him until the last second."

As they turned onto the driveway leading up to the house, two beagles that began barking and trying to bite the tires of the truck greeted them. As they pulled to a stop in front of the house, one of the ladies stood up and called into the house.

"Little John! We got company, come out here and put those varmints in the shed so they can get out of their car!"

Little John and his obviously pregnant wife stepped out on the porch. Little John called the dogs and they followed him to the shed.

A bolt of lightning surged across the sky and there followed a tremendous clap of thunder. The heavens opened up and the rain began to pour down.

Erissa motioned for the men to get out of the car and come up on the porch. "Don't get much company out here anymore," she yelled, "Come on up and watch the storm on the porch with us. It's a lot more comfortable up here than it is in that truck I bet."

Cliff and David hurriedly made their exit from the truck and ran up on the porch. A smiling Lorena said, "Hard to dodge those raindrops when they's so many of 'em ain't it.

"What are you fellas doin' up this way?" asked Erissa. Will you have somethin' cold to drink? I got a fresh pitcher of iced tea in the house if you want some."

"That would be swell", said Cliff.

"Shelly, go on in the house and bring these fellas a big glass of tea...thank you honey."

"That's my granddaughter-in-law Shelly. She's as bout as good as you can be. Sit down fellers and take a load off your feet. My Grandson is sure lucky to have her for a wife, let me tell you. And who might you fellas be anyway?"

"I'm David Spencer and this here is Cliff Myers. We're from over Charleston way."

"I'm Erissa, Erissa Wheeler and this here's my sister Lorena, Lorena McPherson. That feller out there in the shed with the hounds is my oldest son Little John. I had another son named Isaac but he died a few years back. His boy Danny was killed in France durin' the war and he was never right since. I think he just pined away after his wife Julie died.

"My boy Little John's got three kids; all grown now. His wife Melba passed away last June. Shelly is married to his youngest boy Mark and they're gonna have a little one this fall. My Grandson Mark is named after his Grandpa Mark who died in the Civil War."

Shelly emerged from the house with two tall glasses of iced tea. She handed them to Cliff and David who both thanked her. She took a seat next to Lorena who was rocking away in her chair listening to her sister.

"We used to get quite a bit of company up here in the old days. Especially when we made cider; we had so much fun when we were young didn't we Lorena?"

Lorena smiled and nodded her head.

Another bolt of lightning split the air followed by a crash of thunder. Little John yelled from the shed, "I'm headin' in. I ain't stayin' out here any longer."

He rushed out of the shed and ran towards the porch nearly falling as he slipped in the mud.

"That's the fastest I've seen you move in a long while." said Erissa. "Must be the lightnin' that got to you. You used to run faster than that though."

"For cryin out loud Ma, I'm almost 60 years old. Can't run any faster than that!"

"I know son, go on in and get you a glass of tea and come on back out here and sit a spell with us."

"I've seemed to be doin' all the talkin' boys, now it's your turn. Where you from again? What're you doin up here? "

"We're from down Charleston way like I said; Cliff here is the Archivist for the State of West Virginia and I'm with the Kanawha County Historical Society. We are here on a mission. We have some important news for you.

"I understand the McPhersons and the Wheelers had a great loss during the Civil War. We are here to let you know we have found your missing loved ones."

"Erissa gasped and clutched her throat.

Lorena stopped rocking and sat forward in her chair with her heart in her throat. "You found Gabe? He's alive?"

"We found their bodies Lorena. They were killed in battle on top of Kanawha Mountain near Charleston. They were found buried in a cave atop that mountain by an old coon hunter.

He told them the story that Rafe Crawford had told Cliff and all about the Battle of Charleston.

We have their bodies at a funeral home in Charleston. We felt it was our responsibility to find their relatives and get them home for a decent burial."

"You found my Pa?" asked Little John. "I can hardly remember what he looked like."

"We want to bury them right here on the farm, up in the meadow in the little family cemetery." said Erissa, how soon can we get them home?" She looked over at Lorena. "As soon as possible I hope, we've been waitin' on them for a long time."

"We can have them here in a couple of days." Cliff replied.

"Lorena looked at her sister and said, "See, I told you he'd be comin' back to me like he promised me down at Arcadia. His Papaw Isaac told me he would be back. Just like he said, we would be together forever at Arcadia. I want him buried there."

Lorena told the men about Arcadia and how she and Gabriel had met there as children. She told them of the many happy times they had shared there together. She told how the love between her and Gabriel developed and of the promises they had made to each other.

"Little John, would you please help me get Arcadia cleaned up for Gabe? I promised him it would be as beautiful on the day he returned, as it was when he left. Will you help?

"Of course Aunt Lorena, I'll get Mark to help us too. We'll get started on it tomorrow. He should be back sometime tonight. We'll have to dig three graves in the cemetery too. Looks like this rain is goin' to last for a while boys, that road gets pretty bad when it rains. Would you like to spend the night here? It should be clearin' up sometime tonight."

"Thank you Little John, for your hospitality." said David. "If it wouldn't be too much of a burden we would like to stay. We'll even help you at Arcadia tomorrow, Lorena, if you'll have us."

"You're more than welcome," said Lorena, "And your help would be appreciated."

She got up from her chair and walked over to the two men who stood up. She put her arms around Cliff and gave him a hug. She then turned to David and hugged him also.

"I've got to get Arcadia all prettied up for my Gabriel. I promised him it would be as beautiful the day he came home as the day he left. Thank you so much boys for comin' here today. I have been waitin' so long for news of my Gabriel. I knew he was comin' home soon, Papaw Isaac told me so. He said I wouldn't have to wait much longer."

David's eye caught a flash of red from Lorena's breast.

"What a lovely pendant you're wearing Lorena. I've never seen anything quite like that before. It's beautiful!"

"This was given to me by my beloved Gabriel before he went off to the war."

She lifted it up for David to look closer. "You see, it's his heart. He told me that whenever I was thinkin' of him to look at it and he would be thinkin' of me at the same time. It has been a real comfort to me over the years just as it is now."

"I think I will go inside a lay down for a while. I don't mean to be rude gentlemen, but all of a sudden, I seem to be very tired. We'll meet again in the mornin'. I hope you have a pleasant night."

Lorena bid goodnight to the others and went inside.

"Who's Papaw Isaac?" David asked Erissa.

"Papaw Isaac Wheeler was the Wheeler boys' Grandfather. He was the real patriarch of the family. I knew him well. He was sure a storyteller and he sure liked his hard cider. See that keg over there?" She pointed towards the end of the porch. "That's his special keg. He had his name carved on it."

"We used to have such grand times pickin' apples, makin' cider, apple butter and pies back when I was young. We still get a few apples out of the orchard, but most of the trees are gone now. Hardly get enough to make a couple of pies."

"Anyway, there was never a better man than Isaac Wheeler. He'd give you the shirt right off his back if he thought you needed it. His son John, the boys' father, was just like him."

"When we got the word about the boys bein' missin' it was very hard on all of us, especially my Pa. Danny was his only son and he just seemed to pine away after about a year with no word. Ma died less than a month after my Pa. I had the two boys and moved in with Lorena. Life was hard then."

"John Wheeler came over one day with a wagon and said he was takin' us both in over at his house. He said he couldn't stand the thoughts of us women bein' down there alone and tryin' to run a farm. At first, Lorena didn't want to go, but after she did, she was glad she came. We've been livin' here ever since."

"Our house had been in disrepair for quite some time, the roof leaked and it was sure cold in the wintertime, one night it burned down. Don't know how the fire started, wasn't anyone livin' there. It just caught fire and burned to the ground."

She paused for a moment, lost in thought.

"Papaw Isaac kinda went a little crazy right before the boys went off to war. I believe it was his age catchin' up to him. He would say the strangest things sometimes. He would talk to imaginary people and sometimes he would think he was in his youth again, fightin' in the War of 1812."

"One night not too long after the boys left, he got out of the house somehow and the next mornin' they found him floatin' in the water down at Arcadia. That was sure a sad time for both of our families. We buried him in the little cemetery in the meadow and people from all over came to the funeral."

"Wait", said David, Lorena just said that Papaw Isaac told her about Gabriel comin' home! How can that be?"

Erissa smiled and said, "Lorena has had dreams ever since old Doc Philson came by and told us about the boys bein' missin'. She told me that most of the time she dreams about Gabriel, but sometimes she dreams about Papaw Isaac. When she dreams about Papaw Isaac, he comforts her and tells her secret things."

"She says that sometimes when she's down at Arcadia alone he comes to her and talks to her there. I used to try to get her to tell me what Papa Isaac told her, but she would never tell. She said it was a secret. I for one don't believe in ghosts or anything like that, so I figured it was her imagination and if that comforted her, so be it. I never chided her for it."

"I ain't never seen anything strange around here except for one of Little John's coonhounds nursin' a kitten one time. Now that was strange, seemed like that old coonhound adopted that kitten as one of its own. It used to play..."

"Excuse me Erissa," Cliff interrupted. "I don't mean to interrupt you or change the subject, but what can you tell us about the boys? I'd really like to know what they were like."

"Well let me start with my brother Danny. He was from Irish stock and had a tinge of red in his hair. He was always so kind to me and Lorena. He'd do anything for us. He loved to play Town Ball, or Baseball as they call it today. He was very good at it too. He could run like the wind. I used to watch him play at Letart. He loved animals and workin' with Pa. He was my Pa's pride and joy and like I said before, when he went missin', it kilt my Pa."

"James was the oldest of the three Wheeler boys. He took a wife named Maggie just before the war. They had one child named Albert. Maggie died right after Albert was born. James and the baby moved back here with John and Elva. John and Elva raised Albert after James went to war. Albert took a job on a riverboat and died on the Mississippi when the boilers exploded. We got a tombstone over there in the meadow, but his body was never found."

"Mark was the next oldest. He had been courtin' me for quite some time before anyone even knew about it. He was a good man; so strong and carin' for me and the boys. He was tall with golden brown hair and flashin' blue eyes. He had a smile that never left his face. I begged him not to go to join up, but he said he felt it was his duty to go and serve his country just like his Papaw Isaac had done."

She wiped a tear from her cheek. "I cried myself to sleep every night for well over a year after he left. I was fortunate to have my two boys to help me get over losin' him."

"Gabriel was the youngest. He was a good-lookin' boy. He looked a lot like his Pa John. When he was little, he was quite a rascal. Lorena told me many times, about how they met and fell in love down there at Arcadia."

"He loved to hunt and fish. I always thought he was kind of skinny, but Lorena thought he was the handsomest man on the face of the earth. He was so in love with my sister and her with him that they promised each other that they would be together forever, that nothin' would keep 'em apart." She paused. "Then the war came. They were about to marry when that happened. It nearly broke Lorena's heart. James and Mark tried to talk Gabriel into stayin' here, but he would have none of it. He had the same patriotic feelin' that they did."

"The boys had a sister named Rachael and one named Susan. Rachel married a boy named Job Gloeckner and they moved to Louisiana years ago. We used to write each other regularly but I haven't heard from her for quite some time now. I'll have to write her and tell her that her brothers are finally comin' home."

"Susan died just after the war ended. Caught pneumonia or somethin' like that."

"Gentlemen, I'm feelin' a might tired myself. Why don't you get your things and come on in. I'll show you where you can sleep tonight. We'll be gettin' up early in the mornin'. Lorena will want to get started cleanin' up down at Arcadia."

Chapter XXVI
Arcadia / 1925

The old man stopped talking and sat back in his rocker. "Come on Grandfather", said BrieAnna, "tell us the rest of the story."

"Yeah Dad, don't stop now," Amy added.

"I'll go on in a minute, just need to take a bathroom break. Boy, I can't believe this storm. It's still carrying on like crazy outside! He got up from his chair and headed for the bathroom.

"Let's get some more wood John", said Casey.

"Anybody want some more pie or ice cream?" Linda asked.

Every kid in the room raised their hand and yelled, "I do! I want ice cream!"

"I think I'll make a pot of coffee too."

"That sounds good", said Kelli.

The old man returned to his chair, relit his pipe and waited for everyone to be settled again.

Linda walked in and handed him a cup of coffee. He took a sip and continued.

July 19, 1925

It was still dark when Cliff woke up to the smell of bacon frying. He poked David in the ribs and said, "Boy! I have to go to the bathroom. Wake up, don't you smell breakfast cooking?"

David sat up and rubbed his eyes.

"Let's get dressed and see what's going on. How'd you sleep last night?

"Like a baby Cliff. It's so much quieter out here in the country that it is in Charleston."

"I slept pretty well too, said Cliff, "except I had to get up once to go outside and pee. When I was out there, I got quite a scare. I was standing there peeing and looking out towards the meadow. I swear I saw the old man, Papaw Isaac standing out by this tree. I did a double take and then I realized it was a deer. A big one too! It took off and had its white tail raised as it ran away from me. Now I have to pee again."

Cliff waited for David to finish dressing and they walked into the kitchen together. Lorena was setting the table. "Boy that sure smells good!" exclaimed Cliff! "What are we having?"

"I'm fixin' bacon, eggs, taters and biscuits. Do you boys want some coffee or milk?"

"Coffee" they both said at the same time.

"Where's the bathroom, asked David?

"Why, do you want to take a bath, asked Lorena?

"No, I just need to relieve myself."

"Oh", said Lorena, "The bathroom's out back. Go through the front door there and walk around back. You'll see the "bathroom" there." It's a two holer so you both can go at the same time. We're real modern here you know!

She chuckled as she turned back to the stove and began stirring the potatoes she was frying. "Hurry up" she called as they were going out the door, "Breakfast is about ready!"

When the men returned Erissa was sitting at the table. "Where's Lorena?" Cliff asked.

"Her, Little John and Mark went on down to the cemetery in the meadow to pick out where to dig the graves. Mark came in last night; he's really excited about all this."

Shelly entered the kitchen and poured herself a cup of coffee.

"Good mornin'," she said, "Mark kept me up most of the night talkin' about his Grandpa comin' home. He said even though he never knew his Grandpa he had a pretty good picture of what he looked like from the stories you told, Grandma. He said he was feelin' both happy and sad at the same time."

"I think that's how we all feel Shelly," said Erissa, "I'm glad there's gonna be a closure to all of this."

"After you boys have had your breakfast, we'll head on down to the meadow and help the others."

When the men finished their meal, they offered to help clean things up.

"I'll take care of things here," said Shelly, "You all go on down to the meadow. I'll clean up and I'll make you all a good dinner."

"Don't take on too much now Shelly," cautioned Erissa, "You're carryin' my great grandchild. If you get tired you lie down and rest a spell."

"I'll be fine Grandma."

Erissa led the men out the door and headed over to a storage shed. She went inside and emerged with a sickle and a scythe.

"Do you boys know how to use these? She handed the scythe to Cliff, "You got be careful you don't cut your leg off!

"We'll figure it out." Cliff said as he stepped back and took a couple of practice swings with the scythe.

She handed the sickle to David and went back inside. She came out with a rake and shovel in her hand. She handed the shovel to David and put the rake over her shoulder. "Let's go, they're waitin' on us."

As they neared what was left of the old orchard Erissa stopped and said, "Over there is the cemetery."

Cliff glanced to his right and saw Little John or Mark standing beside a tombstone. He had his hand resting on the top of the stone and appeared to be watching them. The distance was too far to recognize which one it was for sure.

"And over that way is Arcadia," Erissa continued. Cliff moved his gaze to the left. "Right over there is where the pathway begins to go down to the creek."

"Should we go over to the cemetery and help Little John or go down to Arcadia and start?" asked Cliff.

"Erissa looked puzzled as she turned to Cliff then glanced over in the direction of the cemetery.

"Looks like they're all down at Arcadia, we'll go there first."

Cliff looked back towards the cemetery. There was no one there. The figure he saw standing beside the tombstone was gone. "I swear I saw Little John or Mark over there." he said.

"I didn't see anyone over there." David said, "You must be seeing things."

They walked through the old orchard and down through the meadow towards Arcadia.

David and Cliff were expecting to see a very beautiful place as they had both formed mental pictures of it from the descriptions given to them by Erissa and Lorena.

As soon as they entered the portal in the underbrush, a zephyr of cool air struck them. It was as though they stepped into an air-conditioned room. The sight they beheld as they walked down the pathway towards the creek amazed them.

The pathway was lined with many multicolored flowers. Streams of sunlight filtered through the surrounding trees and the air was filled with the sounds of bees humming and birds singing.

They stopped and looked around in wonder when they reached the top of the hill overlooking Arcadia.

The pool of water was a beautiful dark green. On this side of the creek was an area of about half an acre. It was covered with grass and looked as well manicured as any mansion yards they had ever seen. There were bushes and flowerbeds filled with all kinds of beautiful plants that had been meticulously cared for.

There were apple trees, peach trees, mulberry trees and cherry trees dotting the area. They were filled with birds, singing and flying from tree to tree. The men marveled at the sheer beauty of this place as they slowly walked towards the flat rock.

On the opposite side of the pool, the woods came almost to the water's edge. There were many different kinds of trees in this part of the forest, Walnut, Hickory, Buckeye, Maple, Sycamore and Birch.

The men could see squirrels running and playing in the leaves that lay on the forest floor. They watched them as they chased each other around and around the tree trunks.

They watched as two little otters wrestled playfully on the far shore, oblivious to the human presence on this side.

They looked towards the left, where the creek came in and formed the pool, there was a huge Weeping Willow Tree. Its draping branches nearly reached across the creek.

Birds of all kinds flittered through the trees and over the water, Cardinals, Blue Jays, Robins and Sparrows to name a few. The men saw flashes of yellow as Finches flew through the trees and from bush to bush.

Humming Birds and Butterflies hovered to drink the sweet nectar produced by the thousands of flowers blooming in the area.

On the bank, just to the right of the flat rock that protruded out over the water, was a huge, stately Oak tree. Its branches hung over the pool and provided shade over the water. One long limb hung over the pool and from it hung a short piece of rope that looked like it was growing from the tree. A little further back, another rope dangled from the limb. It was a lot longer and the men knew it had been placed there so someone could swing on it.

"That rope in front was put up there by my Gabriel a long, long time ago." said Lorena who had walked up to the men, "It broke not long after Gabriel left, but I never had the heart to have it removed. Over the years, the limb sort of just growed around the knot Gabriel tied. We put that other one up there when Erissa's boys were little."

Little John and his son Mark walked over to the men.

"This is my Grandson Mark," said Erissa, "He looks a lot like his Grandpa."

Mark shook hands with the men and gave his Grandma Erissa a hug.

When I came home last night, Grandma and Shelly met me on the porch and told me all about what has happened. When do you think we can get Grandpa and the others back here?"

"Well, we'll head back to Charleston today after we're finished here," answered David, "and tomorrow we'll get started on making the arrangements to transport the bodies. Shouldn't take more than a couple days I figure."

"Doesn't look like we got much to do here." Cliff said, "This place is beautiful, the most beautiful place I have ever seen!"

Lorena said, "We've all tried to keep this place up as I promised my Gabriel and with the help of my nephews and everybody, I think we've done a tolerable good job."

Little John said, "Me and Mark have already cleared out what little brush there was up on the ridge, so I guess we'll work on the cemetery now. Let's head over there and get started before it gets too hot."

Mark added, "We've already selected gravesites for my Grandpa, Uncle James and Uncle Danny. Aunt Lorena wants Gabriel to be buried here."

"That's right", said Lorena, "Were goin' to bury Gabriel right over there where we were goin' to build our house."

Chapter XXVII
The Boys Come Home / Community Hall, Letart Falls

A flash of lightning lit up the house followed by an extremely loud crash of thunder. The old man paused in his story to exclaim, "Boy is this ever going to quit?" This must be the storm of the century!"

"I like it!" exclaimed Amy.

"Well so do I Amy, but I just hate the thought of people getting their basements flooded and such."

"Grandfather, Is Arcadia still there, can you take me to see it" asked BrieAnna?

"Arcadia will always be there," answered the old man, "let me finish my story and you will understand why I never took anyone there."

July 22, 1925

Before the men left Letart Falls on the return trip to Charleston two days ago, they stopped again at the Post Office and asked Grace if she would help coordinate the transfer. They offered to pay for any expenses she would incur including charges for using her telephone to communicate. She readily agreed.

The following morning after their arrival at Charleston David contacted the funeral home and had them seal up the coffins. He and Cliff lined up some volunteers to help transport the coffins to Letart Falls.

The Governor of West Virginia announced that the cost of transporting these men who served their country and the State of West Virginia would be paid for by the State of West Virginia. This would include all the funeral expenses as well. He presented Cliff and David with four American Flags and four State flags to be presented to the family.

This morning volunteers from the Kanawha Valley Historical Society and several others including

Reverend Jamison and the Mason brothers, George and Irvin arrived at the funeral home. George and Irvin had tried to locate Reuben Clark to see if he wanted to come along, but were unable to find him. Reuben's house up in the holler looked like no one had been there for a while. No one they asked had seen Reuben for quite a while. The supervisor at the mine, where Reuben worked sometimes, said he hadn't seen or heard from him in a long time.

The coffins were removed from the Funeral Home and placed in the back of four pickup trucks provided by the volunteers. Gabriel's coffin was placed in the back of Cliff's truck. The trucks were adorned with American Flags and the procession up the road towards Ravenswood was a sight to behold. It was led by the four trucks and followed by six cars.

The plan was for the coffins to be taken to the Community Hall in Letart Falls. The public would be allowed to come there to pay their respects to the families this afternoon and on the 23rd after which the coffins were to be taken to the Wheeler home and a private funeral would be held there on Saturday the 25th.

Erissa and Lorena had asked that only the family and selected individuals be permitted to attend the funeral. Those invited were David, Cliff, Governor Gore of West Virginia, Governor Donehey of Ohio, Officers of the Kanawha Historical Society and the Meigs County Historical Society, Doctor J. R. Philson III of Racine, Grace Roberts the Postmaster and a few friends of the family. There would be about twenty people in all.

As was the custom, local people had already begun to bring food to the Wheeler home. There were pies and cakes of all kinds, hams, fried chicken and casserole dishes.

When the procession arrived at Ravenswood, the Ferry operator was waiting for them. He took the four trucks containing the coffins across the river first and they waited while he went back for the cars.

A crowd was already forming at the Community Hall in Letart Falls when they arrived. They went to the back and unloaded the coffins. They placed them in the center of the auditorium.

Members of the Methodist Church had already set up long tables on each side of the auditorium where people could sign their names in a book for the family and leave flowers or donations.

They had decorated the auditorium with American Flags and red, white and blue bunting. There were already many baskets of flowers. They had been arranged on the tables and around the area where the caskets were to be displayed. The people waiting outside to gain entrance were carrying more flowers.

A table had been set up behind the coffins where Erissa, Lorena, Little John, Mark and Shelly sat to accept the condolences of the many visitors expected.

The news of this event was printed in newspapers all over the states of Ohio and West Virginia and people came from all over both states to pay their respects.

At six that evening the volunteers closed the doors of the Community Hall and advised those still waiting to enter that they would have to come back tomorrow.

Cliff and David stayed the evening at the Wheeler home. The others all went to Racine and stayed in one of the hotels there.

The next morning they were all back to the Community Hall at 7 am. There was already a crowd waiting that was bigger than the day before. There had never been that many people in Letart Falls before.

By noon, the auditorium was filled with flowers and the volunteers began to set them outside. The family members were becoming very tired and took turns

~ 199 ~

taking a break from the endless lines of visitors coming to them with well wishes and condolences.

Around two in the afternoon, a group of men from the Baptist Church Choir in Racine arrived and sat in the shade of a large elm tree outside the Community Hall.

They had brought their guitars, flutes, banjos and fiddles. They began singing songs from the Civil War era. "Aura Lea, Aura Lea, Maid of golden hair", "When Johnny comes marching home again hurrah, hurrah". "We'll rally round the flag boys, rally once again, shouting the battle cry of freedom."

These songs and many more were sung by the men as the people crowded around to listen to them. Their music wafted in through the open windows of the auditorium and filled the air with the sweet, low, sound of their voices, provoking memories in the minds of many people.

The choir began to sing, "The years creep slowly by Lorena, the snow is on the grass again."

Lorena quickly reached into her pocket and pulled out a letter she had received from Gabriel. In this letter, he had told her of the men at Point Pleasant singing "Lorena" for him. He had written down every word to the song.

Her eyes followed the words as she listened to the men singing outside. They got every line correct. When they finished singing, she folded up the letter and stuck it back in her pocket.

She looked at Gabriel's coffin. "Yes" she thought, "The years have crept slowly by, but it won't be much longer my love, until we're together as promised and we'll never part again."

The volunteers closed the doors at 6pm and waited for the people outside to leave. They then loaded the coffins back in the trucks and headed for the Wheeler Home.

There was room enough for only three coffins in the living room. Lorena insisted that Gabriel's coffin be placed in the study room.

The volunteers that brought the coffins were offered to partake of the food that had been brought to the house. They and the family had a fine meal and when the volunteers left, they were all ready to go to bed. The day had been exhausting.

Lorena said, "You all go on to bed now, I'm gonna go in the study and sit with my Gabriel for a while. All of you have a good night." She entered the study and closed the door.

Concerned, Shelly asked Erissa, "Should we let her go in there?"

Erissa answered, "Of course, why not, she's been waitin' a long, long time to be alone with her love. It won't hurt anything for her to spend some time with him in there."

As they all helped clean up the kitchen, they could hear Lorena's muffled voice coming from the study. They couldn't tell what she was saying and thought she must be praying or something. Then they were surprised to hear her laugh. She laughed loud and hard.

"Should we check on her", asked David?

"No!" answered Erissa, "Leave her be! Let's all go to bed. I haven't heard her laugh like that in years."

Cliff and David were lying in bed listening to the muffled sound of Lorena's laughter coming from the study. "I hope she's all right," said David, "this is very strange."

"I'll tell you what's strange", said Cliff. "Lorena has not shed a tear at all. As a matter of fact, when we were taking the coffins into the Community Hall, she was smiling the whole time. Maybe this whole thing has messed up her mind."

"She seems sane enough to me," said David. Perhaps she is just finally glad that it's over and at least she has what remains of Gabriel. You know, people deal with grief in different ways, what seems strange to us may be just her way of expressing her grief."

"Whatever!" said Cliff, "All I know is this is just downright spooky and I'll be glad when it's all over and I can get back home."

Chapter XXVIII
Lorena Reunites With Gabriel / July 24, 1925

The sun had not yet crested over the horizon when Erissa woke up. She hurriedly threw on her robe and went to visit the outhouse. Upon her return to the house, she noticed the door to the study was still closed.

She walked over to the study and pressed her ear to the door. She heard nothing. She gently turned the doorknob and quietly pushed the door open.

The sight, which met her eyes, caused her to scream loudly and pull the door shut. She began to cry hysterically waking up the rest in the house.

"What's wrong!" shouted David, the first one to reach Erissa. He grabbed her and held her with his arms around her shoulder.

"In there! In there!" was all she could say as she pointed towards the study.

Cliff arrived and opened the door. There, on top of Gabriel's coffin lay Lorena in a fetal position on her right side. Her left arm was extended and in her hand was a letter.

David and Cliff went to Lorena and tried to wake her up. "Lorena, Lorena! Wake up!" Cliff brushed aside her hair and was surprised to see her smiling.

"She's dead! David exclaimed when he could not locate a pulse."

"Oh my God!" exclaimed Cliff, "Oh my God!" Clutched in her right hand was the red, crystal pendant; its golden chain hanging from beneath her clinched fist.

David took the letter from Lorena's hand and said, "C'mon, let's go outside."

As they emerged from the study David said, "I'm sorry everybody, I am truly sorry but Lorena has passed away."

He gently closed the study door. Amid the "Oh No's" and sobs of the family members, he said, "Let's all go out on the porch and sit for a while to clear our heads and think what we should do."

The all went outside on the porch and David said. "Lorena had this letter clutched in her hand Erissa, It's addressed to you." He handed the letter to Erissa who nervously opened it. It read:

To my Dear Sister Erissa and family,

Please try to understand. I want all of you to know that I did not take my own life. I knew all along when I was going to leave this world and be with my Gabriel. I was made aware of this a few days before Gabriel came home. I want you to know that where I am, as of this moment is with my Gabriel and I am happier now that I have been in a long, long time. Don't weep for me and don't be sorry that I am gone. Please understand that I am finally where I want to be and I will be happy forever.

I have a few special requests to make to you and I pray that you will please do these things I ask.

Erissa, please, please has them unseal this casket and place my body in it beside my Gabriel. Bury us together in this casket at the spot I showed you at Arcadia. Please put my pendant in the casket with us.

Little John and Mark, after Gabriel and I are buried at Arcadia, go to the flat rock. Dive under the water and at the base of that rock, you will find a large stone about the size of a hen. Pull that stone away from the base. There is an opening there that contains sealed mason jars filled with money I have saved over the years. I don't know how much is there,

I lost count years ago. But it is for you. Use it to keep this house and farm in the family. After you retrieve the money, I want you to let Arcadia go. Let it grow over. Do not allow anyone to go there except the family to care for our grave. Seal off the pathway from the meadow. I know this seems strange, but please, please do this for me.

Remember, don't grieve for me, and be happy. Take advantage of everything life has to offer. Make it beautiful for yourself.

Erissa, my dear sister, I promise you that one day, you and Mark will be together again also. Just have faith that it will happen and it will be.

Your Loving Sister and Aunt,
Lorena

Chapter XXIX
Leave it be!

"That's so sad Grandfather, why did she have to die?" BrieAnna asked.

"Life sometimes causes sadness BrieAnna, but you know what? It also gives us happiness in so many ways. I still grieve for my Mother and Father but when I look at you and all my kids and grandkids, I realize that life has given me so much to be happy about. Lorena is happy now and like she said, take advantage of everything life has to offer and make it beautiful."

"Lorena got her wish. She was placed in the casket with her Gabriel and buried at Arcadia on the knoll overlooking the pool.

When I was about 10 years old, I went to the Wheeler House to visit my Great Grandmother Erissa. I called her Great Grandma Erissa. It was then that she first told me this story and showed me the boxes of letters that the boys had written.

I was enthralled with the story of Arcadia and even though she told me never to go down there, I decided to see for myself what Arcadia was like. I'll never forget that day.

There was a storm brewing and the horizon was filled with boiling black clouds. The maples all had their leaved turned belly up to welcome the approaching rain. My Great Grandma Erissa was taking a nap and everyone else was in town. I thought, "Now's my chance" so I hurried out to the orchard and across the meadow.

I walked along the line of brush that rimmed the meadow looking for the opening down to Arcadia. As I was walking along, I suddenly heard laughter, children's laughter. I followed the sounds and found an opening in the brush. I slithered in and started making my way down this path.

All of a sudden, there was a tremendous crash of thunder and the air seemed to be filled with electricity. I thought for a moment that I was going to be struck by lightning or something. I started on down and fell a few times. The wind was blowing fiercely.

The path through the brush led me to the top of a small hill and as I looked down at the creek, I saw two children, a boy and a girl standing on a flat rock protruding out over the creek.

They were staring at me. I started to say hello when they started throwing rocks at me and yelling for me to get out. The little girl threw a rock and it hit me on the shoulder, then bounced up broke my glasses and cut my ear. I put my hand to my ear and felt the blood.

I got scared and ran back to my Great Grandma Erissa as fast as I could. My yellow t-shirt was covered with blood and the rain started pouring down before I got to the house. I slipped and slid in the mud so many times that my blue jeans and sneakers were caked brown with mud by the time I got there.

Grandma Erissa asked me what happened and I told her about those mean kids down by the creek who hit me with a rock.

She smiled and then said, "I told you not to go down there didn't I. Maybe you'll listen to me now. You got no business down there." She cleaned up my ear and taped my glasses back together. "Don't ever go back there again!"

When I was a young man in the service, I came home on leave one time. My Great Grandma Erissa had died a few years after my first visit and I decided to go back down to Letart Falls and see the cemetery where she was buried along with all my ancestors. When I got there, I found that the road up to the house was almost all washed away. I had to park on the main road and walk up.

It was sad to see the old house nearly all caved in. Not much left of the beautiful farm I remembered as a child. The meadow was all grown over, covered by bushes and weeds so high that it was hard going.

I made my way through the meadow to the little cemetery. It was overgrown also. I cleaned out as much as I could and promised myself that I would return sometime and clean it out really well. I paid my respects to my Great Grandma Erissa and the others buried there.

As I was leaving, I decided to try to find Arcadia again. Even though the experience I had the last time I tried to find it was still in my mind and the fact that my Great Grandma Erissa told me never to go there, I remembered the story she told and my curiosity got the better of me.

I walked to the other side of the meadow and tried to find an opening through the dense underbrush. As I walked along, I got the eeriest feeling that someone was watching me. I turned around quickly and about fifty yards from me was an old man, leaning up against a tree. I could see his white beard.

I turned to continue my search and as I did, he was suddenly standing right there in front of me. The hair on the back of my neck stood straight out as I gazed into the eyes of that old man. They were the deepest blue I had ever seen. He was dressed in the oddest clothing! His gaze was fierce and foreboding. I started to say something like "Hello" or "Hi," but he spoke first. He said, "Leave it be son, Leave it be!"

Embarrassed and a little frightened, I averted my eyes and looked down at my shoes. When I raised my head to ask him what he meant, he was gone. In that instant, he had vanished.

I was so shaken by that encounter that I took off running through the meadow back towards the house. Three deer bounded out of the tall grass along the edge of the meadow and took off running right behind me. I thought they were chasing me. I kept on running even when I reached the house. I ran all the way to the car. I fired that engine up as quickly as I could and got out of there. I haven't been back to this day.

I will never go back there and I want you all to promise me that you will never try to go there. Over the years, I have concluded that Arcadia is a special place meant to be only for Lorena and Gabriel. It is not for us to intrude upon their Paradise. I took what the old man said to heart.

"Leave it be son, leave it be!"

About the Author

C. Stephen Badgley was born in Letart Falls, Meigs County, Ohio. When he was eight years old, his family moved to Tuppers Plains, Ohio where he lived until he graduated from High School. He entered the U.S. Navy and became a Hospital Corpsman. He served as a combat medic with the 26th Marines in Viet Nam. Upon leaving the service, he attended Mountain State College in Parkersburg, West Virginia and then entered into the Trucking industry. He and his wife Linda now reside in Canal Winchester, Ohio. He is the father of two lovely daughters, Kelli Anne and Amy Jo. He has two grandchildren, Casey and BrieAnna. His main interests in life are history, genealogy, Ohio State basketball, football and fishing.

Steve, as he prefers to be called, is also the author of the books, "Where the Lilies Cry", A Point of Controversy and is currently working on a Civil War novel to be entitled "Opequon."

Thank You

We hope you enjoyed this book. Please visit our
website for other great stories.

WWW.BadgleyPublishingCompany.com